ROGUE'S RUN

Galactic Gunslingers 1

Lara Santiago

MENAGE AMOUR

Siren Publishing, Inc.
www.SirenPublishing.com

A SIREN PUBLISHING BOOK
IMPRINT: Ménage Amour

ROGUE'S RUN
Copyright © 2009 by Lara Santiago

ISBN-10: 1-60601-508-7
ISBN-13: 978-1-60601-508-7

First Printing: June 2009

Cover design by Jinger Heaston
All cover art and logo copyright © 2009 by Siren Publishing, Inc.

ALL RIGHTS RESERVED: This literary work may not be reproduced or transmitted in any form or by any means, including electronic or photographic reproduction, in whole or in part, without express written permission.

All characters and events in this book are fictitious. Any resemblance to actual persons living or dead is strictly coincidental.

Printed in the U.S.A.

PUBLISHER
Siren Publishing, Inc.
www.SirenPublishing.com

DEDICATION

Dedicated with much gratitude and appreciation to my great friend, fellow author and all around awesome brainstorming buddy, Emma Wildes. I adore our fabulous chats where we discuss pretty much any subject ranging from the writing life to life in general. I love that we became fast friends in the early years of our careers and I especially love that you came up with the awesome title of this book, Rogue's Run. You're the best.
Thanks, Em.
Lara Santiago

ROGUE'S RUN
Galactic Gunslingers 1

LARA SANTIAGO
Copyright © 2009

Prologue

Abigail Deveronne had been convinced that marriage to Myron Smedly was the worst thing that could possibly happen, until she woke up next to his dead body.

Five days into a very unsatisfactory marriage arrangement with a man old enough to be her grandfather, Abigail ran like an evil entity chased her from the deplorable marriage bed she'd endured. Her destination, the only other home she'd ever known and current residence of her beloved aunt Eugenia, was not far away. Unfortunately, it also housed her former guardian, Pitney, the man who'd chosen Myron as her husband.

The crackling sound of the light orange grass poked angrily through her thin house slippers as she dashed madly through the pre-dawn morning to escape. She ran from a situation she fearfully acknowledged she'd prayed for more than once in the past five days.

Not for Myron's death, but for freedom from him.

Passing the large amethyst crystal rock formation marking the entrance path to her destination, Abigail kicked in some reserve strength, racing to the front door of her sanctuary.

Aunt Eugenia would know what to do. The vision of being enfolded in her aunt's comforting lemon verbena scented embrace empowered her to beat fists on the door until a servant finally opened it, but barred her entry. She was left on the doorstep to wait until the "master" could be fetched even though she specifically asked for her aunt.

Waiting impatiently, shifting from one foot to the other, she happened to glance over her shoulder noticing two of Segoha's three moons in the starry dark sky. The twin quarter crescent moons, one stacked on top of the other, didn't shed nearly enough light to keep her fright at bay.

Pitney came to the door wearing his usual black garments in the form of a robe. He always wore black, the predominant color of conservative clothing in their religious sect, but his usual neat appearance was marred. Hair askew, he had tufts of the graying mass standing up all over his head. "What is wrong with you, Abigail? Why are you beating on my door at this unholy hour?"

Abigail tried to speak, but instead started crying. Pitney released a long angry sounding sigh. After a moment, she managed to whisper, "Myron is dead."

Pitney's eyed widened. "What?"

"He's dead," she said it again and stepped forward to enter the house, but Pitney hadn't shifted in the doorframe. He still blocked her entrance.

Instead of moving to invite her inside, he closed his eyes as his teeth ground together hard enough to make a squeaking noise. "Go back home this instant."

Abigail sniffed in surprise. "But couldn't I see Aunt Eugenia for just a minute? Please?"

"No. Go back to your home and wait for me." He slammed the door in her face.

Abigail stared at the door in shock for one endless minute before shuffling off the porch. She'd hoped to be escorted from the cold doorstep and into the receiving room for comfort. When her parents had been alive, they always entertained guests in the receiving room whether the guests were welcome or not.

There was no comfort forthcoming from Pitney. Abigail wasn't surprised as she and her former guardian admittedly had never gotten along. Her persistent rebellious streak was the cause of much discord, according to Pitney.

Abigail sniffled, wiped her eyes on her robe sleeve and made her way back to Myron's house. This time she strolled instead of running as darkness still pervaded the early morning.

Once she stood before Myron's ramshackle little house, she couldn't bring herself to enter. Instead, she waited for Pitney on the broken down porch.

He arrived as dawn broke over the distant jagged mountains of her home planet Segoha.

Wearing his signature black robes with his hair combed hastily into place, Pitney stomped onto the porch. "What did you do to him, Abigail?" he shouted in a fury of accusation.

"Noth…nothing," she stuttered.

Pitney flung the front door open and strode into Myron's house as she followed with reluctance. She suppressed a shudder as she crossed over the threshold and into the formal living area. It was no surprise Pitney blamed her for this unfortunate event. She'd lived with his barely concealed tolerance of her existence since her parents died eight years before.

"I woke early to do my chores and he was not, not moving. I didn't know what to do so I ran to—"

"Yes, yes I know about that part. Running like a frightened child to my house. I simply don't know what you hoped to accomplish by dragging me into this. You should have thought things through, Abigail."

"But I—"

"But nothing. Hush and let me think. Why couldn't you have waited two more days?" Pitney asked the wall as he paced across the well-worn living room rug. Abigail didn't know if he spoke to her or not, so she remained silent. He acted as though he expected her to reside with a dead body for two days before reporting it. Not likely.

The fond memory of her loving parents was always tainted by their choice of her guardian. In the rigid canon of the Saints of Aria, women had a specific role to fulfill. According to Pitney, it was the way the holy writings intended men and women to live. Love played no part in marriage. To wed was solely for procreation and in order to accomplish this, love wasn't required.

Although, Abigail's mother had been at liberty to choose a husband she cared about, such was not *her* fate. Her mother and father shared a rare love match. However, Pitney had very harsh opinions regarding her parents' union.

Since she'd been old enough to understand what marriage was, Pitney preached endlessly his disapproval of love as a reason to wed so she rarely brought it up. He made it clear he would not allow Abigail the same freedom enjoyed by her mother.

Abigail glanced around the living room which had become her home a mere five days before. Myron's house was nowhere near as grand as the one she'd grown up in.

The depressing décor washed over her again in pathetic waves as it had the first time she'd seen it. The day she'd been married off to an old man. The day her dreams of love had died in her marriage bed.

She hadn't been allowed to make the house her own. If she'd had any say in the décor, she would have pitched everything inside out the front door.

Myron had grunted a few words of foolishness and folly over buying anything new when the threadbare rug and limp curtains remained, in his opinion, still serviceable. New furniture? A wasteful endeavor, best forget any notion of luxury. Abigail spent the first five days trying to come to grips with the new life thrust upon her.

Her new husband, Myron, was not a communicative man. For the most part, Abigail felt like a piece of the threadbare furniture waiting for him to gesture, or more likely grunt, his requirements. At least until dusk. Abigail dreaded bed time most of all.

Myron never spoke. Never kissed her. He merely reached for her in the darkness beneath the sheets, used her for a few minutes and rolled away snoring before a minute was gone. Every single time. Abigail shivered in memory of the past five days and nights.

"This is a disaster," Pitney muttered more to himself than to her, shaking Abigail from her miserable reverie. He paced for several more minutes before reaching into the deep recesses of his dark overcoat to procure a device. The square black box with buttons covering one side wasn't allowed as regular use by members of the Saints of Aria. Usually, a forum was called when an SOA member required communication with Outworlders. And even that was a rare occurrence for private citizens.

She knew about the device Pitney held from the lectures on evil in her discipline classes. He could contact other planets with it. She watched in abject fear as he proceeded to push several buttons hoping that if he got caught, she wouldn't be jailed for being in the same room.

Pitney spoke in low tones into the device, but Abigail heard several key words and phrases that did not bode well for her uncertain fate. She heard the words, "Raylia…proxy marriage document…dowry payment upon confirmation of signed papers…"

In the end, Pitney didn't even wait an hour before arranging her remarriage. Her next intended husband resided at the far edge of the Ksanthral system on a planet called Raylia where yet another Saints of Aria sect dwelled. Pitney spent mere minutes negotiating a quick contract, including a dowry for her next husband living across the far reaches of space.

Pitney turned to see her perched on the sofa as surprise registered across his stern features. He'd probably forgotten she wasn't a piece of furniture, too.

"Go to your room," he commanded.

Abigail surely blanched and shook her head. "But *he's* in there."

Pitney huffed. "Then go to the spare room. Just leave my

presence." He turned away and pushed more buttons on the illegal black device.

Ten minutes later Abigail sat in the cheerless extra room as instructed and thought further about the unfairness of her life. The rebellious streak she harbored flared hotter and brighter the longer she sat immobile in this stifling little space. She stood suddenly unable to remain seated a second longer and took a step closer to the door. Without a plan fully thought through, she decided to leave even if only for a few minutes.

"Disobedient" was the only recognizable word circling in her brain.

Slipping out of the spare room against strict confinement orders was likely a punishable offence, but she didn't care.

Abigail made her way quietly to the formal dining area where the opened wedding gifts sat. Tradition, in their sect, dictated the abundant gifts would remain displayed until the first week of marriage had passed. Giddy elation at her current defiance gave her strength to move forward.

The well-known tradition was one she'd been informed of repeatedly by the sour female relatives of her intended, Myron. These were same sanctimonious biddies who'd readied her for her wedding night. Only they hadn't mentioned in any detail what she could expect on her honeymoon. They only said it was her duty to submit and that she should endure whatever came to pass in silence and dignity.

Dignity played no part of her wedding night and the only silence was hers. Thank the saints above, she bore that night all in complete darkness. It was easier to tolerate *that* which she could not see.

Her eyes were wide open now. Because the marriage to Myron hadn't lasted a full week, Pitney had the power to renegotiate another husband for her. She also suspected it was a way the stingy could recoup their wedding gifts if the marriage didn't last.

Tradition or not, Abigail decided she had earned one or two of the bounteous gifts for being introduced into the marriage bed by a loudly-grunting, smelly old man.

Standing at the edge of the dining area, Abigail listened for her guardian's voice. Watching the doorway, she pocketed a few valuable trinkets, hiding them in the deep folds of her gown as self justified repayment for the wedding night she'd endured and the following nights as well. The memory made her shiver in revulsion even now.

As a school girl she'd wondered about what went on between a man and a woman behind closed doors. At the age of sixteen, she'd gotten a forbidden glance first-hand of the sex act between the attractive stable hand and the woman who cooked her guardian's meals.

When Abigail grew older, she'd fantasized about that memory repeatedly. She hadn't thought she needed any explanation for her wedding night. However, after her experience with Myron, sex wasn't something she ever wanted to participate in again. Neither was another husband so soon after the first. Even as Pitney now contracted transportation for her new marriage. Myron's body hadn't even cooled. But as a woman in this world, her choices were limited to none. Her rebellious streak at an end, she decided not to anger her guardian further and crept back to the empty extra room.

Pitney strode into the spare room only seconds before she returned from the dining room.

"I've arranged for you to leave within the hour. You will go to Raylia and meet my representative, Mr. Jorge Smith. Then you'll present yourself before the Common Guild and a new husband will be selected for you. Try not to kill the next one off so quickly."

"Why do I have to leave the planet?"

He glowered at her, but she didn't look away. The rebellious streak reared and Abigail kept her gaze locked on his.

"Do you want to go to jail?" Pitney leaned forward. He towered over her as if to dissuade her from further argument.

Rebellion, still coursing hot and wild through her veins, kept her from being even the least bit daunted. "No. Why would I have to?"

Pitney's face froze into a mask of displeasure. He didn't speak for so long, she thought he might not answer. "Don't you think there will be questions as to why your husband died so suddenly?"

What? "I didn't *do* anything to him."

Pitney shrugged and a smug smile stretched across his thin lips. "So you say. But will you be believed?"

Abigail hadn't even considered she'd be blamed for his death. She'd heard lots of stories growing up about what sinful women did to their pious husbands and the punishments they suffered.

Ultimately, Pitney was correct. In a test of wills, she'd be blamed for any wrongdoing regarding Myron's death. But a worst thought occurred to her. "What about Aunt Eugenia?"

Pitney's smirk dissolved into puzzlement. "What about her?"

"Do I have time to say goodbye?" Abigail hated to beg him, but desperately needed to hug her aunt one last time before leaving the only world she'd ever known. "Please?"

"No."

Beastulio. The vile curse word flashed in her mind unbidden.

Abigail's lips tightened and her face screwed up as insolent thoughts of disobedience washed over her. Unfortunately, Pitney witnessed her defiant expression before she could hide it.

His eyes narrowed. "If you do not get yourself to Raylia post haste, I'll see to it that your precious Aunt Eugenia is placed in the most despicable elder house I can find. I'll be checking to ensure you arrive at Raylia in one month's time, or else you'll be responsible for her fate."

Abigail swallowed her anger in the face of her sweet simple Aunt being sent away from the only home *she'd* ever known and locked into a desolate place unfit even for rabid animals.

Modern technology did not interfere much with the ideology of the Saints of Aria. In the distant past their religion hadn't accepted machinery which could be operated without manual labor. Over the centuries little by little, some machinery became incorporated as the men required the ability to produce more than the strength of a single back alone could accomplish.

This philosophy translated to elder house facilities as well. The threadbare home she'd shared with Myron would be considered a palace compared to the finest elder house on Segoha.

"Please let her stay in your home. I'll go willingly to where you direct."

Pitney's self satisfied smirk did little to assure her, but she wasn't about to let Aunt Eugenia suffer if she could stop it.

A gleam in her eye, Abigail did send up one final prayer of spiteful attitude for Pitney. She fervently prayed he would one day be forced to spend his final days living in the very elder house he'd threatened her aunt with.

Pitney deserved it, her aunt did not.

* * * *

A furious woman was best avoided at all costs. Jesse Pelland recently learned this practical advice first hand from his ex-wife. Unfortunately, the angry female stranger currently in his path couldn't be dodged. She owed him money and Jesse needed the funds with a desperation he didn't want to amplify with hard feelings.

Eyes flashing her palpable wrath, Greta raged, "You reneged on our deal!"

"Did not." From across the small clearing on the furthest and most desolate moon circling planet Raylia, Jesse studied his patron and hoped to resolve this brewing conflict without bloodshed. Especially without any violence to *his* person.

Tired from his recent journey performing a task he hadn't enjoyed, Jesse dearly wanted to get back to his ship, *Dragonfly*. Beyond the fact that this remote part of the universe wasn't the safest place to be, Jesse was weary all the way to his bones and ready to get back home.

The short range shuttle craft he'd come to this rendezvous with was currently hidden a few kilometers away. But it wouldn't endure an intense scrutiny. Jesse didn't want to get stuck on this barren rock if anyone with theft on their mind discovered his hiding place.

Greta screeched and put Jesse's attention back where it belonged. Her fists clenched at her sides, she ground her teeth making a squeaky noise loud enough to be heard across the clearing. "But you didn't kill him."

Jesse shrugged. "Didn't need to."

Greta's hand came up and pointed a stiff glove-covered forefinger at his face. "I wanted him stopped."

"And he is."

Her face upturned to the sky briefly before dropping to level another fury-filled stare his way. "I wanted him dead. He deserved it. You know what he did." Spittle had collected at the corner of her thin-lipped mouth and distracted him for a moment in disgust.

Shaking off his unease, Jesse got serious. "Deserved or not, you didn't specify dead. You said stopped. And he is. I want the agreed upon bounty. Now."

"You're a coward," she spat out the accusation and took an angry step closer.

"No." Jesse pulled his Infiltrator revolver out slowly and pointed the large bore barrel at the ground. "I simply didn't add another perished soul or a murder to my already dark conscience. The job is done. Your target is finished in all matters that are important. Now pay up!"

The unhappy client glanced at the gun in his hand and deflated a little. Even though he currently had it set for "stun," Greta obviously understood the power of the weapon resting alongside his leg.

The other two settings were "maim" and "kill" and she couldn't tell where the firing mechanism was positioned. To rile him into pointing his gun at her was a foolish endeavor. She pushed out a deep breath either to calm down, or possibly in resignation, Jesse didn't know or care. He simply wanted to get paid.

Moments later she extracted a bundle from the pocket of her oversized skirts and threw the tan drawstring pouch overhand directly at his face. Jesse caught it easily in the palm not occupied cradling his weapon. He holstered the gun and pulled the drawstring cords open to study the gems inside. Poking his finger down into the bag to ascertain they were real, he grunted in satisfaction.

Perfect. He had his payment. Time to go.

Jesse lifted his head to say a sarcastic thank you very much, but the plain-faced woman in the endless layers of black Pilgrim skirts was already gone.

Good riddance.

While Jesse had approached this meeting with all the enthusiasm of a criminal racing to his own execution, the way back to his space craft, *Chaser*, was a gleeful gambol. Like almost every habitable planet in this galaxy, there was little water and lots of space dust. He was thirsty, but didn't want to even take the short time to stop and take a swig from his canteen. Already late in returning from this compulsory mission, he longed have his life back.

Lola waited for her blood-money payment and she was not by nature a patient woman. It would be a miracle if she hadn't already ruined his meager financial gains or his business credit by now. He pressed on knowing he'd done the best he could given very limited choices. And he still had a long way back home.

While he'd made the journey to Raylia in good time, he didn't expect his return would be as fast. He'd pushed the limits of the small craft but hoped the *Chaser* would hang together long enough to return.

Once back on familiar ground and secured inside the small cabin of his short range shuttle craft, Jesse eased the priceless gun back into its precious case and swore, for a second time this century, he wouldn't ever retrieve it. *At least not without due consideration.*

He buckled himself into the pilot's seat of his shuttle and readied for take off to meet the *Dragonfly* waiting what seemed like half a parsec away. They weren't truly that far but the journey back would take a few days and given the limitations of his shuttle, it would seem much longer.

Stroking the console as it powered up and hoping the aging shuttle would make it safely back to the base ship, Jesse allowed his thoughts to slide into his past.

Fifteen years ago he'd worn the custom-made and government issued Infiltrator revolver weapon proudly. He protected his small fraction of celestial space as one of the universes most respected law enforcement division, the Galactic Gunmen. Promising to bring civil order to a universe gone wild, he worked hard to rid the lawless planets in the Ksanthral system of bad men. He'd worn his Galactic Gunmen badge with pride. During that time long ago, he'd been blatantly naïve to presume that "might makes right." And ultimately foolish.

He learned the eventual truth, of absolute power corrupting absolutely, the hard way.

While he hadn't participated in the events that brought that doomed-from-the-start organization to its knees, he certainly lived with the consequences every day of his life thereafter.

Eleven years ago, after the GG Infiltrator revolvers had been banned from use or existence, Jesse decided quietly to keep his in a safe place for the uncertain future. By refusing to hand the weapon over, and insisting that he'd destroyed it to keep it out of the wrong hands, his punishment for protocol violation had been severe. It had taken him another eight years to scrape any kind of decent life together after forfeiting his pension for failure to surrender his "lost" weapon.

Those were the rules. He made his choice long ago. Now and again a stream of news would report the recovery of a previously unreturned Infiltrator revolver. They always made the mainstream news. The most powerful smart weapon ever conceived, the GG

Infiltrator could scan a human mark as far away has half a click and regardless of where the muzzle was aimed, once fired, it would hit the specified target. Every. Single. Time.

Dangerous in the hands of the wrong kind of man. Tremendously dangerous in the hands of one thousand men not vetted for zealous psychotic enthusiasm.

The galactic unified government had procured and produced one thousand of the next generation weapons to bring a warring galaxy back from lawless chaos. Until several powerful members of the Galactic Gunmen carrying them had gotten out of control with the power hungry need to rule. The manufacturing plant had been destroyed by extremists the day after shipping the one thousandth revolver. They didn't seem so extreme when the truth about several criminals carrying the Infiltrators came to light.

The galaxy force condemned all of the Galactic Gunmen to unemployment. Something great became a threat of the worst kind and what they came to fear. In the end, the GG Infiltrator revolvers were summarily outlawed and the Galactic Gunmen were disbanded.

The last count of sophisticated Infiltrator weapons Jesse had heard bandied about was thirty five. Counting Jesse's weapon put the tally at thirty six. However, he suspected several more "lost" weapons hid in secret places out there somewhere waiting for discovery.

Jesse hoped no one ever found out about the sin of his youth, the prideful crime of keeping the most dangerous weapon ever made. He couldn't be the only one who'd done so. He spent a brief moment in reverie over his proudest achievement in being accepted as a Galactic Gunman and on its heels came his darkest moment when the whole fucking mess fell apart.

While he understood that might didn't make right, Jesse also knew that a fire should be fought with fire.

Thirty six reported missing or lost Infiltrator weapons were far too many still loose not to have a backup plan. Or, he thought with cynical amusement, the minimum ability to fight equally with the inferno of power the outlawed guns possessed.

He rechecked his instrumentation again, sent up a fervent wish into the universe that he'd make it back to the Dragonfly without incident and blasted off of Raylia's most distant moon.

An hour into his long flight, he realized that the universe wasn't currently answering any wishes and this was about to be a longer and more peril-filled journey than he'd planned.

Chapter 1

Planet Delocia Space Port, one month after departing Segoha

"The thing is, Miss Deveronne, I've got as much money as I need. What I *don't* have is access to regular feminine companionship, you understand."

Abigail took a deep breath to keep the distain from her tone as she spoke to the distorted screen of the vid-phone. "Mr. Horace, if you'll forgive my candor, I'm not looking to be anyone's companion—feminine or otherwise—and besides, as I explained, I don't have any money in my possession."

"If you think I'm giving up the accelerator module for Dooley's ship for free, you're crazy."

She sucked in a quick breath. "Of course not, but please allow me to continue my journey and I'll see that funds are sent directly once I arrive at Raylia."

"No. I get paid up front or no part."

"Please, Mr. Horace. I need to be on time to my destination." *Aunt Eugenia's safety depends on my timely arrival to Raylia.* The one month arrival limit in place to ensure her complete cooperation never left her mind for long. Landing on Delocia had not been planned and Abigail feared she was already dreadfully late for her meeting on Raylia. She sniffed to deter the sudden urge to sneeze and adjusted herself in the dirty seat doing her level best not to touch anything in the dusty, deplorable office.

Being sent across the galaxy to an unknown stranger to acquire a second husband after already being married to a man old enough to be her grandfather was also the second worst thing that had ever happened in her short life. Although, this current conversation was running a close third on her top five list of bad situations. Even as desperate as she was to continue her journey to Raylia, she didn't wish to give up her body to do so.

"One hour of your feminine companionship while you do everything I want you to...or no deal."

Beastulio.

Abigail didn't know what disconcerted her more, the sexual demands he made or the fact that his vid-phone was broken and she couldn't see what the depraved reprobate looked like. She pictured a greasy old man in dirty ragged clothes rubbing his crotch every five seconds to assure himself his package was still intact.

"Then no deal." Abigail pushed the disconnect button to end the call. Resting her chin on her palm, she pondered what in the world she was going to do now. Being a feminine companion, even for an hour, wasn't an option. She shuddered at the thought of sex with yet another grizzled old man.

* * * *

Jesse Pelland cursed a blue streak as the *Chaser's* engine belched smoke and coughed fuel into the atmosphere of the unidentified planet he flew over. He'd babied the fuel regulator on the trip back to his space cruiser hoping to make it there for repairs. Being at the mercy of whatever godforsaken Allied Supply Hut squatting on the nearest backwater planet he was about to crash land on didn't thrill him. The fact that he would be even later to his next rendezvous hammered his brain with deplorable possibilities.

"Delocia Space Port. Downtown Delocia Common." He read aloud from a star chart listing viable planets in the Ksanthral System. Sounded ancient. They'd probably charge him triple if they knew how much money he carried. Shit, they'd probably charge him triple no matter what they thought his financial status was.

To even his odds, he'd have to hide absolutely everything in the secret compartments of the hold and change into his most raggedy clothes before heading to the nearest available Allied Supply Hut. And that included hiding his prized Infiltrator revolver as well. He surely didn't want to take the chance of it being seen or losing it to a gutless wanna-be gunslinger on a dusty nowhere planet.

Jesse hit the ship to ship communicator button and called his engineer on the *Dragonfly*. "Tiger? Come in, Tiger. This is Pelland."

"Tiger, here. What's up, Captain?"

"The *Chaser*'s engine is crapping out as we speak. I'm leaking fuel and probably leaving a trail of parts in my wake. I'm gonna have to land on Delocia for repairs."

"Roger that." Tiger didn't hide the amusement in his tone.

Pressing his fingertips near an eyelid to stem a sudden tick which fluttered beneath the thin skin, Jesse asked, "You got something to say?"

"Don't let 'em charge you *too* much now." Tiger laughed out loud into the speaker and added, "Put your old shabby clothes on or you'll pay out your ass for parts."

"Yeah. Yeah. I know how it works. I'll call you when I'm on my way again."

"Roger that…and, Captain? You got a…well, I guess it's sort of like a message. It's right here…um…waitin' for ya."

"Fine. I'll deal with it when I get back. Pelland out."

Tiger sounded like he wanted to say more about whatever the message was, but Jesse didn't want another problem weighing on his mind. He had plenty on his plate at the moment. Not the least of which included an ugly landing with an engine about to crap out miles above a planet he didn't want to land on.

Once he got back to his cruiser he could arrange payment on the debt he owed, get back that important document he treasured representing his freedom and still have a nice stash of cash. But first he had to get there.

The shuttle belched again and leaned sideways. Jesse tried to straighten the craft for landing, favoring the aft side as he put the ailing ship down for a hard landing on the barren wasteland of Delocia.

* * * *

Abigail contemplated her rock or hard place options sitting before the blank vid-phone several minutes later. She was interrupted from her melancholy thoughts by Dooley, the captain of the derelict spaceship her guardian had hired to escort her to the planet Raylia and her next husband.

Dooley appeared at the door to the communications room where she sat pondering her miserable life. He'd been contracted by Pitney after her first husband died. She wondered how her guardian had known about the horrid transportation services Dooley provided.

He sauntered into the room giving her body an intense scrutiny as he always did. Dooley was yet another depraved reprobate on her journey to Hades.

Eyes riveted to her bust line, he scratched his crotch and asked, "Did Horace have the accelerator module I need for my ship?"

Abigail turned her gaze away. "Yes. He has it."

"Great. When are you gonna go get it?"

"I'm not. He's demanding sexual favors in return for the part. I refused. We'll have to think of something else."

Dooley barked out what she assumed was a laugh. "Nope. That won't work."

Abigail closed her eyes and counted silently to three. She opened them and fixed a glare on Dooley. "Why not? Surely there are other supply stores available?"

He shook his head fiercely. "Horace is the only game in town, sweetheart. He always gets what he asks for. An authorized Allied

Supply Hut is the only supply business that's allowed this far out in the solar system."

Abigail thinned her lips into a frown. "Well, he's not getting what he 'asked' for from me."

Dooley crossed his arms over his well sized mid section. "Guess we'll be staying here on Delocia for a spell then."

She straightened her spine. "You contracted with my guardian to take me to Raylia to be presented before the Common Guild. My future husband waits for me there. I can't be late or else…well, never mind. I must get there promptly."

Dooley zeroed his focus on her breasts again and muttered, "Don't see the hurry in getting you *there*."

"What?"

"Nothin'," he mumbled. Dropping his arms, Dooley scratched his crotch absently. "Besides, it don't matter what was contracted. I told your guardian, Pitney, I'd do my best, but I can't get you to Raylia without the accelerator module."

"Why is it my responsibility to get the part?" Abigail huffed. "It's your ship that's broken!"

Dooley sighed as if she were an incompetent child and explained, "Horace is the only one with the supply parts. And he don't want anything I've got to trade. That's why I had *you* call on the vid-phone." He winked before dropping his gaze to her breasts for a third time. She noticed with disgust that the speed of his crotch scratching increased. "I knew he'd trade with you."

Abigail crossed her arms in embarrassed anger to keep from launching at him with fingers stretched ready to throttle him. He'd only take it as a proposition anyway. "It's still not my responsibility."

"Listen, lady, I'm fine to stay right here on Delocia. You're the one all fired up to get to Raylia. You want off this fuckin' rock…then you'll halfta trade with Horace. Like I said before, he don't want what I'm offerin'." Dooley kept scratching his crotch during his impassioned speech. Abigail was disturbed to notice a growing bulge there.

She looked away quickly as if the sight might blind her. "It was made clear to me that I must arrive within a month to Raylia to meet my obligation. I won't disrespect the Common Guild and my next husband by being late to this appointment." *And I must save my Aunt Eugenia from the elder house.*

"Then I guess you'd better pretty yourself up and go get that part." Dooley licked his lips as his gaze traveled up and down her body. He backed out of the communications room. The tent at the front of his trousers left little to the imagination of what he expected to happen between her and Horace.

Beastulio.

Abigail wished for the courage and the knowledge to shoot the crystalline handled revolver hidden in the folds of her long gown. A wedding gift she'd relished having appropriated before the funeral and well before Myron's greedy family took everything else.

Perhaps if she pointed it at Horace's forehead he wouldn't notice that she didn't know how to pull the trigger.

Chapter 2

Jesse secured the *Chaser* after changing into more casual clothing. Within the cargo area of the craft, he kept a small four-seat land rover vehicle for local on planet travel. He drove it into the small desolate encampment of downtown Delocia Common after stowing every morsel of valuable property, including his Infiltrator revolver, in the secret compartments of his hold. They were uniquely hidden and even the most advanced penetrating radar would not see his concealed cargo. His cruiser, the *Dragonfly* had similar compartments only they were much larger. Jesse used them for smuggling when legal jobs in the galaxy became scarce.

He'd smuggled a couple of people, trying to avoid the Ksanthral Alliance, across the galaxy once. It was a worrisome practice and not something he'd try again. The chance of death by suffocation was too high. If the occupants in the hidden cargo hold ran out of oxygen during the flight, there was no way to communicate. He normally stuck to inanimate objects for cargo. Less trouble anyway.

Spotting the tavern called "Wet Yer Whistle", Jesse parked his vehicle and headed in that direction. Best to get a lay of the land before embarking on any trips to the parts store. He'd been to plenty of backwater planets just like Delocia in his travels as a supply transporter. Most were the same across the galaxy, but a few weren't what they seemed. Better to figure out how things worked before blundering in and making an irreversible mistake.

The stinging memory of a very recent occurrence slid into his mind as Delocia's constant wind blew fine dust into his face. He blinked and rubbed dirt around his eyes. He'd get his part, fix his shuttle and get the hell out of here. He probably should have sent for Tiger and his cruiser, *Dragonfly*, but Jesse didn't want his valuable ship anywhere near this planet if he could help it.

The whole place screamed of desperation.

Jesse didn't want to deal with desperate people today. Or endanger his ship needlessly.

He entered the bar, which miraculously enough looked exactly like every other dirt-water space bar he'd ever entered. It was identical right down to the ramshackle corrugated metal walls and dim lighting. It even smelled the same. Stale beer stench, tobacco smoke residue and the sour undertones of vomit permeated the air.

"What'll ya have?" the bartender asked as Jesse ambled slowly to the cheap tin topped bar lining one side of the seedy establishment.

"Whatever's on tap." Jesse stuck his thumb on the payment pad and held in his grimace at how many credits he'd just spent for the cheap liquor he was about to consume. Or not.

The bartender placed a glass of frothing amber and green swirling liquid before him and remarked, "Haven't seen you around these parts before, have I, stranger?"

Jesse answered carefully not wanting desperation to color *his* tone. "Been meanin' to stop by for some time now and took the occasion to check this place out for future transport business."

"Transport business? Guess you'll need to register with the local Delocia Bureau of Transportation for a license."

"Right. Where are they located if ya don't mind sharin'?"

The bartender tilted his head to the left. "End of the street. Can't miss it."

"Oh," Jesse snapped his fingers as if the idea had just occurred to him, "I'd better find a local Allied Supply Hut while I'm here. Never know when I'll be needin' parts." *Like right now.*

The bartender's eyebrows lifted in seeming understanding. He nodded once in the opposite direction of the Delocia Bureau of Transportation. "That's Horace's shop at the opposite end of town."

Jesse lifted his drink off the bar. "Thanks for the information." He took a drink grateful that he'd spoken before consuming the rot gut beverage. He was fairly certain his vocal cords dissolved with the first sip.

He smiled at the bartender who thankfully moved away to serve another customer, missing Jesse's true grimacing reaction to the drink. He slid his tongue around the inside of his mouth to ensure his teeth hadn't melted and pretended to drink another sip before sliding away from the bar to head for Horace's supply shop.

Jesse didn't need to get a license for commerce on this rock. He wasn't ever coming back here once he got away. The sooner he got off of this dusty desolate planet, the better.

Conscious of his time running out, Jesse put urgency in his step as he hurried down the wretchedly poor streets of Delocia. He side-stepped more than one poor soul cowering along the street on his journey for a fuel regulator.

The stench of urine and unwashed body odor was appalling as was always the case when the huddled masses of humanity congregated in public places. He walked faster as if his own hard-won life from streets like this was in jeopardy.

Seeing the red and yellow sign stating "Allied Supply Hut" ahead dislodged the painful childhood memories from his mind. Time to get off this rock for good.

Jesse opened the door to the Supply Hut. A bell jangled on the door as he entered yet another dark space and squinted to see the layout or anyone present. When his eyes adjusted enough he could see he stood in a small reception room of sorts with an empty desk and a few assorted chairs against one wall.

Directly before him was the open yawning doorway to a long dark hallway. Positioned next to the desk, it drew him forward. "Hello?" he called out to the darkness. Nothing.

"Hello, anybody here?" Jesse listened intently. Nothing. He sighed out loud. He hoped this wasn't going to take forever. He needed to get his part and get going.

Looking behind him once, he entered the dark space noticing diffuse light to the left at the end of a fifty foot hallway. He passed what looked like office doors, four on each side, and he traversed the dark hall slowly. He hoped no one waited in the shadows to surprise him. He wished he'd brought a weapon, but didn't want to stir up trouble if it wasn't needed.

Arriving at the end of the hall, Jesse turned and leaned to the left to find the source of light. There was another shorter hallway perhaps twenty feet. Now he could hear voices raised in anger coming from the end of this hall and a brighter light source.

The heated argument between two men led him silently down the second hallway, this one without doors, to a wider brighter open entryway on the right. He turned and a large open room filled with several rows of ceiling to floor shelves and lots of parts greeted him.

Jesse didn't see anyone, but heard an angry male voice proclaim, "…you greedy idiot. That wasn't the deal. I go first or I won't share her—"

The man's impassioned speech was cut short by the sound of a gunshot. Jesse started to move forward, but a sharp pain to the back of his head stopped him. The second blow landed him on his knees and he blacked out.

* * * *

Jesse came awake slowly. The pounding ache in his head made him want to throw up. He coughed and the pain of it made him suck in a deep breath and crunch his eyes closed against the light showing red on the inside of his eyelids.

He dreamed while he was unconscious. Bad dreams. Dreams of his hungry past directly after his parents had died leaving him alone and destitute.

Seeing the poor folk on the streets of Delocia had likely prompted the painful memory of his past. He coughed again and stirred awake to escape the demons of his past only to be slammed with a bone jarring headache banging relentlessly in his brain.

Opening his eyes only a slit, he realized he was on his back resting on the hard floor of the bright space he'd entered with the shelves of parts. He sat up, tried to grab his throbbing head and noticed the gun. It was in his hand. Even as heavy as it was, he'd almost hit himself in the temple with the stupid thing.

He put the gun down on the floor by his hip and put a hand to the back of his head discovering two lumps on his noggin. At least he wasn't bleeding from them. He glanced at his time piece realizing only twenty minutes had passed since he'd entered the Supply Hut.

Squatting on the balls of his feet, he tested his ability to stay vertical before attempting to rise all the way to a standing position. The faraway sound of a door startled him. He soon heard someone approaching from the hallway just as he turned and noticed the dead body across the room.

Jesse registered the single bullet hole in the forehead of the unfortunate old man along with a pool of sticky-looking blood accumulated near his neck. Then he realized why someone had put the gun in his hand. His DNA would be all over the handle. He was being framed, damn it all to hell. Time for him to get out of here.

He scooped up the gun and stood on wobbly feet. He placed his empty hand on the counter to steady himself when the black splotches of unconsciousness tried to drown him. He tucked the gun under the counter before he hit himself with it. Leaning heavily without a clear memory of getting behind the tall wooden barrier, he readied himself to impersonate the proprietor of the Allied Supply Hut. He'd get rid of whoever was about to enter, figure out how to get out of the mess he woken up into and hopefully do so without going to jail.

Jesse hoped it wasn't someone familiar with the owner of the establishment…or worse, the sheriff raiding the place for an arrest.

Delighted surprise registered when a woman stormed in from the hallway. She was young and very beautiful, which in his case often meant trouble.

The delectable scent of her made the initial introduction and breezed into his face. His libido stood up and took notice. More trouble for him, though the pain in his head seemed to diminish each time he inhaled her fragrance. Her strawberry blonde hair twisted up into a bun secured at the back of her head. Her eyes, a sea green color, complemented her hair beautifully. Then he saw her freckles. She had beautiful freckles sprinkled deliciously across her nose and cheeks.

Freckles were his personal downfall.

Looking at her hair again, he fantasized to himself that her strawberry blonde locks cascaded to her waist once she let it out of the tight twist. Did she have freckles all over? He tamped down his fantasies to see what she wanted. He'd been in a big hurry to get out of here ten seconds ago to nurse his abused head, but he didn't feel so bad now. It was amazing the ails an intriguing woman could cure with her smile…and freckles.

"Can I help you?" He gave the gorgeous young thing his most engaging smile. He realized as he studied her, he'd gone way too long without the comfort of a woman.

Chapter 3

Abigail stomped into the Supply Hut main room after traversing the rat's maze entrance. She bolstered her courage and prepared not to allow Mr. Horace the chance to speak until she'd had her say. She was ready to let loose her planned speech from first tart word to last.

As she walked, she practiced her impassioned diatribe. *I'll shoot you dead before I have sex with you to get his part, you letch. I want off this disgusting planet, but I'm not sleeping with…* And then she saw him.

The words dried up in her throat. She did too want to have sex with him whether or not he gave her an accelerator module in return. The visage of the grizzled greasy old letch she'd pictured with every furious step she taken to arrive here evaporated. In its place was conjured the most attractive man she had ever had the pleasure to lay eyes on.

He smiled and said, "Can I help you?" However, Abigail was stunned into speechlessness.

Dark tanned skin, with sun streaked light brown hair, he'd look dangerous if he weren't gifting her with a seductive smile. And he was tall, very tall. Her shoulders barely came up to the counter while she could see his entire chest above it. His shoulders were impossibly wide. Saints above, did he have a dimple when he smiled? She discovered she was a big fool for dimples.

Reality set in. What was she thinking? She traveled urgently on her way to Raylia and another arranged marriage, which aggravatingly enough, came with another husband. She couldn't be contemplating sex with…this gorgeous man. Could she? He reminded her vaguely of the stable hand she'd watched cavorting with the cook, only this man was much more attractive.

The striking stranger had spoken when she stormed in. She missed whatever he'd said over the pounding in her ears. Her blood hammered through her veins pulsing with anticipation. She swallowed her prepared speech and allowed her lips to soften and shape into a smile.

"What can I get for you, Miss?" he asked with a grin. He obviously missed the angry expression on her face when she entered as if he were distracted. A good thing since it gave her a chance to get her balance. If she had to have sex with someone, this man before her wasn't the worst she'd already pictured.

Abigail cleared her throat as daintily as she could and said, "I need an accelerator module, please. Didn't I speak to you on the video phone a short while ago?" *Please let it be you.*

He shook his head. "Oh no, sorry, that wasn't me. Must have been the owner." The gorgeous man glanced to his right and then back at her with a smile. "I don't work here…uh…exactly…full time. Which craft was that accelerator module for again?" He focused his gaze behind the tall counter for a second before connecting with her eyes once more.

Abigail sighed, completely deflated. Of course the attractive desirable man wasn't the one she got to have sex with. She'd get the owner she'd spoken to. The unseen grizzled greasy man in some back room scratching his stinky crotch in readiness for an hour of her feminine companionship. *Beastulio.*

He glanced at her face and waited patiently for her answer. She cleared her throat again. "For the Rebel Class Star Cruiser."

His mouth shaped into a charming grin. He chuckled, "That old hunk of junk? It needs an accelerator all right. You should accelerate *that* piece of shit into a junk yard. Someone is pulling your chain, Miss. An accelerator won't help that bucket of bolts."

Abigail took a deep breath as her eyes narrowed in suspicion.

What was going on here? Another ploy to extract more than one hour of feminine companionship time for his disgusting boss? "Is that so?" She frowned and crossed her arms ready to do battle.

He sobered as soon as she stiffed her spine. "Listen ma'am," his large calloused hands came up in front of his chest in an I-give-up gesture, "I'm happy to give you the accelerator, but what that old ship needs is a crusher at a recycle center."

"Give me?" Abigail asked her spine snapping a little straighter. "You'll just 'give' me the accelerator? For what additional compensation in return?"

"I'm sorry?" His eyes squinted at her in genuine puzzlement. He looked confused, but Abigail wasn't falling for his innocent act. She knew she'd have to pay. Some way, some how, she always had to pay. Unfortunately, it was apparently never going to be with someone gorgeous like him.

"On the video phone, whomever was here," she said and arched an eyebrow. "The owner requested something specific from me, but not money or credits."

"Oh?" He smiled as if he'd just figured it all out. "Well, okay then. I'll take whatever you agreed to. Allied Supply Huts do lots of trade and credits aren't always what's exchanged." His charming grin made heat rise in her cheeks and a rush of moisture accumulated between her legs. She almost looked down at her body in surprise. That kind of tingly arousing blast had never happened before.

"Really?" Abigail sucked her lower lip between her teeth and chewed lightly in equal parts of anticipation and dread. She wasn't in the habit of having sex with strange men. Especially to get parts for some piece of "shit," bucket of bolts, star craft that wasn't even hers. However, if this was the man she would trade sex for parts with then perhaps she'd change her mind and accept the previously negotiated terms.

"Sure. These sorts of trades are very common."

One hour of her feminine companionship in exchange for one

accelerator module. Fixating on his dimple a moment, Abigail decided she was getting the better part of the deal.

"I see. Well, give me a moment to think."

His eyebrows went up as if surprised, but he said, "All right. Take your time." His patience disarmed her final reluctance. Pitney hadn't had much patience to spare for her in the years after her parents died.

Abigail glanced at the handsome man again. Perhaps it was her curiosity of wanting to try sexual intercourse with someone other than Myron. Her first husband certainly hadn't been anywhere close to her dream man. The sex she endured on their wedding night had been an embarrassing two minute affair leaving much to be desired on her part.

Abigail eyed the stranger's engaging dimples and decided she wanted him. She wanted to trade sex for a part as long as it was with him and not the faceless degenerate she'd negotiated this deal with.

It wasn't like she was a virgin and besides she wasn't exactly looking forward to Raylia and yet another unknown husband. The second one might be even worse than her first. She shuddered inside.

Perhaps this was the singular chance she'd ever receive to experience sex with someone desirable instead of an old stinky man.

She took a deep breath to calm her rioting emotions and with it came a delicious faint masculine scent. Anticipation curled along her spine and sent a pulsing jolt of desire between her legs. Her decision made, she relaxed a notch.

Abigail glanced at that dimple once more and then slid her gaze to his beautiful brown eyes. For once in her miserable life she decided to do something against the rules. Something wild. Something her rebellious streak absolutely demanded. One hour of feminine companionship where she would do anything he wanted. She shivered in anticipation.

Would sex with Mr. Gorgeous be different? She couldn't see behind the counter, but suspected based on the size of his hands his apparatus would be larger than what she'd already experienced. She'd overheard two women on Dooley's transport ship discuss information to determine how big a man was below his beltline without removing his pants. Large hands apparently translated to other large body parts. The very thought made heat rise in her cheeks.

"Where would we do this…um…trade? Please don't say right here," she spoke the words in a rush of embarrassment.

He looked around the large room nervously before planting his hypnotic gaze on her. Why was *he* nervous? Unless he wasn't supposed to partake of the owner's feminine companionship.

"Do you have private quarters?" Abigail looked around as if someone might be listening. "Somewhere else we could go?" She knew she sounded paranoid, but didn't want to be caught in *flagrante delicto* with this man on the premises, no matter how attractive he was. Then again what did she have to look forward to? Nothing.

"Well. Sure. I have a small shuttle with private quarters parked outside of town." His eyebrows scrunched as if he didn't quite understand her reluctance.

The sound of a law enforcement siren in the distance made them both jump in surprise.

"My place it is. Let's go then." He winked at her and moved a step back.

"Don't forget to bring the accelerator module with you," Abigail said. He nodded and reached under the counter and grabbed a piece of complicated looking machinery.

Tucking her needed part under one arm, he turned and disappeared down the first row of shelving closest to them. Moments later, he emerged with another small engine part clutched in the hand carrying the other item. He shot around the end of the counter where the opening was and grabbed her arm with his free hand. She noted that he seemed even taller standing beside her.

The delectable scent of him belied the tattered clothing he wore and unruly hair she itched to touch. She expected unwashed body odor, but instead she got another rush of a musky masculine scent tinged with a clean fragrance assailing her as he led her through the darkened hallways and out on to the dusty street of Delocia Common.

The law enforcement vehicle passed them and darted around the corner down the alley between the squat tin buildings. The gorgeous stranger seemed to relax a little, but Abigail was a bundle of knots.

What am I about to do in the name of rebellious curiosity?

Saints above, what if someone saw them leave the supply hut together? She looked around furtively as he led her down the street praying Dooley and all members from the ship she traveled to Delocia on weren't anywhere in the vicinity.

His hand squeezed her forearm leading her a short ways down the street. Abigail took another deep breath as his scent assailed her. She was very wet between her legs. A hunger like she'd never felt before crept into her lower half with hard anticipation and sensitized the skin beneath her dress everywhere. She craved sex with this man. Was this what desire felt like? Was this attraction?

Perhaps it was time to find out first-hand. No one would ever have to know. The memory of the sexual tryst she'd watched at the tender age of sixteen darted through her mind.

The memory of the stable hand, Dustin, as he'd pumped his lengthened man part repeatedly inside Mary made a blush come into Abigail's cheeks even now.

Mary had writhed and moaned in pleasure at what Dustin did to her nude body. Dustin's tanned hands rubbed Mary's lush breasts and pinched her brown nipples until she cried out. He had chuckled and bent to kiss Mary's mouth as he increased his thrusts. Mary had tightened her legs around Dustin's naked hips.

Abigail remembered the sculpted muscles of Dustin's backside, which bunched and squeezed as he pumped his hips forward into Mary faster and faster until he also cried out and soon after collapsed on her breathing heavily. The two lovers hugged and held each other in a sated sweaty clasp until Abigail snuck out of her hiding place unnoticed.

She had never told a soul about that day. She'd also never forgotten it. All her life Abigail had wanted to experience the same pleasure at the hands of a gorgeous man. She hoped to fulfill her dream with the attractive man now leading her to his private shuttle.

Anticipation drilled through her at the possibilities of the coming hour.

Chapter 4

Jesse didn't know what in the two mooned world this woman wanted to trade for the hunk of worthless machinery under his arm, but he didn't take the time to discover the mystery once he heard the law enforcement siren.

She probably had some antique trinket tucked away in the folds of her pilgrim skirts ready to give him in *trade*. He'd noticed she was dressed as if from the last century, just like the other various pilgrims he'd seen on his extensive travels throughout the Ksanthral system. A recent occurrence flashed in his brain in the form of an angry client named Greta back on Raylia, and he dismissed it. Her cultured speech gave away her religious status more than her dress.

The Saints of Aria lived a simple life, but they weren't stupid. They often used the high-brow kind of speech that made everyone else feel uncultured. The woman before him exuded regality in waves, but not in an annoying way. She was beautiful. High class. Intelligent. Sexy. To top it all off, she smelled like a lazy afternoon in bed complete with satisfaction and rumpled sheets.

He snatched the fuel regulator part he needed for his ship in the shelves of the Supply Hut and the accelerator module she claimed to need. Her part surprisingly had been right under the counter. He didn't stop to ponder the coincidence. Better to get her out of here and sort it all out at his shuttle.

For a female in this desolate outer planet, she was a drink of unexpected frigid water on a hot day. Beautiful didn't even begin to cover what this woman looked like, even covered in the miles of layered fabric she wore. He didn't even know her name.

Coming to his senses, he calmed down. This wasn't a date. It was a business arrangement. Of course, since he traded for stolen goods, perhaps it didn't qualify as business.

He'd swap whatever *trade* she had under the miles of petticoats she wore for the piece of crap he'd just stolen from the Supply Hut. Horace, the owner, wouldn't need it any longer. If, in fact, the dead man sporting the hole in his head was Horace. Ultimately, Jesse didn't care.

Clutching her soft upper arm and very aware of his hand resting next to her breast, Jesse let out the breath he hadn't meant to hold.

He opened the passenger door to his vehicle and tucked her and her voluminous skirts inside trying not to shut the fabric in the door. It'd only take him five minutes to get back to his shuttle.

Jesse spent the short trip thinking about how long it would take him to install the fuel regulator. He also pondered how delectable his passenger smelled and how long her hair was out of the twist. Glancing at her profile he swore those freckles called to him.

He should drop her off at her bucket of bolts ship and hand her the worthless part with his best wishes, but if she were with the passenger cargo crafts as he suspected, they resided in the opposite direction of his shuttle.

One crisis at a time, he thought, inhaling deeply to calm himself. The lungful of air did nothing to calm his nerves since the scent of her came with it. Honeysuckle. His cock flared in desire with every luscious breath.

She seemed very nervous and spent the short trip looking over her shoulder. He didn't take the time to wonder why.

"What's your name, ma'am?"

Her breath caught in her throat. She smoothed the fabric on her skirt before answering softly, "Abigail."

"I'm Jesse. Pleased to meet you."

She glanced at him and her brows furrowed. "Likewise, I'm sure."

"We'll be at my shuttle in a minute."

"Fine." Her fingers clenched each other. She seemed overly anxious.

Jesse stopped trying to make polite conversation. She didn't seem interested anyway.

He parked his vehicle behind the shuttle and pushed the remote to open the hatch. Driving the rover inside the small bay, he promptly hopped out to help her from her side of the vehicle. Again the bounteous petticoats filled the door of his rover until she exited. He didn't know how she tolerated all those layers of fabric in this dry, dusty heat. But the thought of her *out* of those skirts put his head in a direction he did *not* need to go.

She wasn't here for his pleasure. Although her mere presence was very enjoyable.

Grabbing the two parts from the back of the vehicle, he walked her into his shuttle bay and closed the back hatch. Stepping through the main hatchway, her clothes completely filled the door. He shook his head at his errant thought of asking her if she'd be more comfortable without all those skirts and petticoats.

"Is this more what you had in mind as privacy for the trade?" he asked.

She turned to face him as a blush came up in her face. "Yes. Thank you."

The pink in her cheeks highlighted all those sexy freckles he needed to ignore. Why was she so nervous and blushing all of a sudden? Ah, he knew why. She was a pilgrim of sorts. There were probably all sorts of rules about her being alone with a man who wasn't a relative.

Jesse knew very little about the Saints of Aria's culture except that he wanted no part of it. Too restrictive. He hoped being alone with her for longer than two shakes of a lamb's tail didn't constitute some sort of binding engagement.

That would be just my luck.

On his way to pay off one debt to obtain his freedom, only to end up engaged to a tight-laced girl with freckles who smelled like sunshine, fresh honeysuckle and rumpled sheets, wasn't in his recent plans. Of course, he could think of worse fragrances.

For example, fire and brimstone, like Lola.

"Well, let's see what you've got." Jesse wanted to get this deal over with. He still had a fuel regulator to install before he could get off this desolate rock.

An errant thought buzzed around in his head that he couldn't quite latch on to. It was like he'd forgotten something, but he couldn't come up with anything he'd overlooked. He was, of course, very distracted by a certain luscious female crowding the small space of his shuttle.

The elusive, nagging thought kept circulating, but he ignored it in favor of the prim little miss standing before him. Her shy smile already made him nervous.

Abigail looked around his small shuttle as if searching for something as another pretty blush rose in her cheeks. "Is there somewhere I could go…in private…to um…get ready for the trade?"

"The only other room is my private cabin where I sleep." He nodded once to the door behind her. "You're welcome to it."

She must have her treasure tucked up under her skirt in one of the hundreds of folds. Probably she'd have to dig for an hour to retrieve it.

Casting her eyes to the floor, he heard her respond with a quiet, "Thank you," before twisting away from him slowly.

Jesse needed those freckles, and her distracting scent, out of his shuttle. "I don't mean to rush you, but it won't take you too long, will it?"

"N…no," she stuttered. She turned to push through the entrance to his bedroom almost tripping over her skirts and the door behind her as he rolled his eyes. He soon heard rustling and shuffling about in his cabin.

God in heaven, he didn't need to be picturing her pulling up her skirts to look for the trade item. It was probably some wooden trinket her great granddaddy carved and handed down for generations and meant everything to her family. Whatever it was, he'd find a way to give it back without insulting her. He would send her on her way with the worthless accelerator module, compliments of the unfortunate Horace of the Delocia Supply Hut, and his own best well wishes for her continued good health.

After more than ten minutes of him pacing trying not to picture her silken legs, or her hair undone, or her freckles, she called to him through the door. "I'm ready to trade now."

Jesse waited for her to come out. When she didn't he cautiously approached his room and knocked quietly.

"Come in. I'm ready."

Entering his private room, Jesse's warning radar came on as he saw that she waited for him on his bed. Her loosened hair was out of the previous twist and his fantasy was fulfilled. Her strawberry blonde locks went all the way to her lovely smooth ass.

She also happened to be as naked as the day she was born.

* * * *

Illicit thoughts ran through Abigail's mind as she'd taken all her clothes off and let her hair down. She wanted to experience a sexual encounter in the manner she witnessed years ago. However, this time she wouldn't be hunkered down behind a horse stall in the barn.

Jesse hadn't requested her this way, but she was very excited by the possibilities. Sex with someone different. This hour was to satisfy her curiosity nothing more. A sexual experience with an attractive man she desired. Then she'd fulfill her duty and go to Raylia. Aunt Eugenia still depended on her to do the right thing. And she would do the right thing, but not until after she enjoyed the hour with Jesse.

He opened the door soon after she called him. She leaned back on his bed wishing for some sort of blanket to cover herself with, but this was better. He could see what he was getting. She positioned herself exactly as Mary had before Dustin had disrobed. Abigail's skin burned in desire as illicit thoughts of being discovered naked pulsed through her veins.

Jesse's eyes widened in obvious shock when he entered his room. His smoldering gaze swept from her eyes, to her breasts and finally to the spot between her legs before snapping back to rest on her face. Was he disappointed or excited?

"What…what are you doing?" he stuttered.

Abigail resisted the urge to leap up and cover herself. She took a deep breath, expelled it completely and remained still. "This was the agreed upon trade. One hour of feminine companionship for the accelerator part," she said quietly. "I'm ready to do whatever you wish."

"One hour of…" Jesse closed his eyes and put a hand up on the door frame, but didn't move. He cleared his throat and opened his eyes again. His gaze traveled hungrily down her body and back to her face again. She smiled at him for encouragement.

He didn't move from the doorway. "Listen, I didn't expect…that is to say…" he let out a deep breath. "You don't have to…"

Abigail sat up on the bed as her face heated. She'd been foolish. He didn't want her. She voiced her worst fear of being completely unappealing to other men. "You don't find me attractive."

She covered her breasts with one arm as her legs slipped over the side of his bed. She pointed her face to the floor and a sob rose in her throat. "I'm so sorry." Tears fell and she swiped at them with her free hand. What would she do if he didn't trade?

Crossing the room in two strides Jesse squatted before her. He draped a warm hand on one of her shoulders the heat of which sent a tingle down her spine. His other hand tipped her quivering chin up to gaze into his soulfully beautiful brown eyes.

"You have nothing to be sorry for, Abigail." He sighed sharply as if in disgust and added, "For the record, I'd never trade sex for a part.

I'd have simply given you the accelerator module. I'm sorry the owner tried to take advantage of you. He's a sorry bastard."

She gave him a watery smile, "I wouldn't have done this with anyone but you."

His gentle smile vibrated through her. "Thanks. That's nice of you to say." His fingertips massaged her shoulder slowly. Lazily. Distractedly. His gaze locked with hers and a rash of wild thoughts entered her mind.

Memories from what she'd witnessed prior to the act in the barn slid into her mind. The stable hand, Dustin, had kissed Mary very passionately for several breathless moments before the act had commenced. The two had groped and grabbed at each other almost desperately until Mary had taken her clothing off one piece at a time as Dustin had watched with a hungry expression in his lusty eyes.

Kissing intrigued Abigail. She'd never had a real kiss. If she got nothing else from today, she wanted at the very least…one passionate kiss.

"Will you kiss me? Please. Just once," she whispered. *Please say yes.* She leaned forward in preparation ready to persuade him.

His pupils widened at her request. "Well, maybe just one." He leaned forward until only a breath separated their mouths. "Spirits of heaven, you're beautiful," he whispered and placed his warm firm lips across hers. His tongue skimmed across her sensitive bottom lip.

Abigail's mouth buzzed the moment his lips touched hers. His fingers tightened on her shoulder as his other hand slid around her head to rest at the back of her neck pulling her more securely against his mouth. Her body was a mass of prickling sensation. Another pool of moisture gushed between her legs as she opened her mouth against his lips. She touched her tongue to his.

The electric sizzle of the contact made her shiver in desire. Jesse groaned and in the next second his tongue shot inside her mouth with decided thrust to tangle with hers.

Indescribably wicked sensations marched across her body. She trembled, she wanted him so much. An intimate encounter for her own gratification and memory.

No one would ever have to know.

Abigail placed her hand on his chest and then did something she'd seen years ago. She slid her hand between his legs and grasped the stiff, lengthening piece of his anatomy she wanted buried deeply inside of her and squeezed.

Jesse made an inhuman noise so she stroked his penis once again and it pulsed in her hand through the fabric of his trousers. He pushed her back on to the bed and followed her down. She squeezed his cock again and felt her cheeks heat at using the coarse word even in the privacy of her own mind. She'd heard the term "cock" on her travels here and using it silently made her feel even more wicked. His tongue, which already danced in her mouth, became more aggressive thrusting and dueling. Her breathing was out of control.

Trapped beneath him, Jesse continued kissing her and pressed his hips forward towards the very wet place between her legs. She slipped her hand to cup his butt pulling him forward opening her legs in invitation for his advances. His cock seemed to be growing to an incredible size as he moved against her.

Jesse rolled off of her slightly and trailed a hand down between their bodies. She expected him to undo his trousers and a thrill ran down her spine. But instead he placed his hand between her legs and she felt his fingers part her most intimate folds.

She thought he merely assessed her readiness for him. She *was* absolutely ready. His fingers slid inside her body and a moment later his thumb stroked a place, which brought the most scandalous feeling of pleasure she had ever known.

He continued to stroke that one spot until she trembled in anticipation of something stupendous building within her core. He broke the ravishing kiss and his mouth trailed to one of her breasts. The moment his lips clamped over one nipple and sucked hard, a rapturous sensation exploded inside her body radiating from where his fingers still stroked and stroked and stroked. She arched her back unable to stop her contortions of bliss. A shriek escaped from her lips at the sheer volume of pleasure that erupted from her center and radiated across her body in waves.

Jesse kissed a path to her mouth and touched her lips with his again, softly this time. He peppered sweet kisses across her lips as she moaned and trembled from exquisite release.

Chapter 5

Jesse, awash in the scent of aroused female, tried to come back to reality and calm his libido. She'd shrieked her climax and he'd almost come in his pants. In his mind, there was nothing so grand as the sound of a woman being pleasured to release. Especially when he made it happen.

A glimmer of gentlemanly intent wafted through the haze of sexual longing to voice the reason he shouldn't be doing this. He hoped she didn't still think he expected payment for the part.

She moaned, sending any rational thoughts out of his head.

Resting on his side, his face was buried in the soft expanse of her throat. The fast breathing coming from her lips fluttered the hair on his forehead. A moment later her hands were on the move. She trailed fast fingers to his trousers and began opening his belt. When he heard the zipper open, he knew he lacked the willpower to stop the inevitable regardless of her reasons for being here. Her bare fingers stroked his cock almost innocently beneath his under shorts and he couldn't think beyond sinking deeply into her recently satisfied body.

Jesse hooked a thumb into his waistband and lowered his pants enough to free his cock. He shifted his body and rolled on top of her. She suctioned her mouth on his in a deep kiss thrusting her tongue between his lips. Her legs were spread wide open for him so he grabbed his cock, directed it into her very wet opening and obliged her.

The vice tight grip as he slid his dick all the way to connect with her womb sent his body into a nirvana-like shudder at the blissful sensation.

Jesse pulled back slowly and thrust deeply again. And again. He reached to cup her bare breast lightly pinching her stiff nipple as he palmed the perfect mound. She moaned again and her hips arched beneath him to meet each push he made into her sweet body.

The release he sought was elusive. It had been a long time since his last such encounter and he paused to enjoy the pulse quickening feel of having his cock immersed in a tight feminine sheath.

Abigail was still fastened to his mouth, her tongue thrusting in the same rhythm as he pierced her. Mewling noises came from her throat. Her hands clung to his shoulders squeezing and massaging while her fingernails lightly scraped his skin.

He trailed his hand to between them and rubbed her clit as he pushed deeply again and again.

She broke the carnal kiss and shrieked his name as she climaxed. Her pussy clamped down on his cock squeezing rhythmically until he couldn't hold his release any longer.

Jesse pulled back enough to stare deeply into her eyes for his final stroke. He was about to climax. He wanted to watch her face when he did. The sight of her moist swollen lips from their ardent kisses made him shudder with pleasure, but not as much as those sexy freckles across her pert little nose. Her satisfied gaze sent him directly over the edge.

A growl issued from his throat as he plunged his cock to the hilt and released all the pent-up desire he'd accumulated in the short time he'd known her. He decided straight away one time in bed with her wasn't going be enough to satisfy him.

The orgasm wrapped around his cock in a blissful vibration that shot up his spine. He lasted only two more strokes before he collapsed on her, drained completely. He still wore most of his clothes and wished he could feel her flesh against his. He nuzzled her neck and expelled the breath he'd held to experience the release.

Enfolded around each other still breathing hard several heart pounding minutes later, Jesse contemplated his actions and immediate future concerning a beautiful stranger with irresistible freckles.

"What did you do to me?" Her quiet question filled with wonder made him smile. "It was so wonderful." He hoped she meant making her climax.

Sobering quickly he said, "I took advantage. I didn't mean to go so far. You're much too tempting."

Her throaty laugh surprised him, but not as much as what she said next. "I wouldn't have let you stop."

He lifted to gaze to very innocent light green eyes. A grin split his face and he chuckled. "No?"

"I've never felt anything like that. Thank you." She reached a hand to his face and stroked his cheek.

"Where I come from a man isn't much of a man if he doesn't pleasure his woman during the most intimate of acts." He stroked her breast with tender fingers until her nipple hardened.

"I wish I could go there." The wistful tone of her voice brought him back to reality. He shouldn't have had sex with her. She was a pilgrim...of sorts. He'd probably just condemned himself to a life of servitude in marriage. Time to set things straight.

"Listen, Abigail. I don't want to give you the wrong impression about what happened between us and—"

"You still have half an hour left."

"What?"

"You still have half of my feminine companionship time left for the trade." She sighed a contented breath and asked, "What would you like to do next?"

"I didn't do that for the trade. Truth be told, I did it because you touched me and I should have resisted, but I didn't. I couldn't."

Her grin was infectious. "Will you touch me again? I liked it."

"I probably shouldn't." *But I want to.*

Abigail kissed his neck and five seconds later he had both hands on her breasts squeezing and rubbing her nipples as he kissed her lips with abandon. Her hips lifted against his cock which got hard instantly. He released her, stood up and backed away from the bed a foot or so.

The frown registering on her face turned into a grin when he started shucking his clothes off. This time he wanted to feel her silken skin against his.

He was an idiot, but those freckles called to him demanding his attention. He wanted to hear her scream once more in climax. Besides, according to Little Miss Prim and Proper, he still had half an hour left.

Jesse slid his body up hers until he covered her. Her legs shifted out from underneath him to wrap around his hips, putting his cock at the entrance of her very wet pussy. Exactly where he wanted to be. Her hips wiggled as if impatient so he penetrated her. She was tight surrounding his cock with the most delicious heat.

"Want to try something different?" he asked.

She didn't answer right away, but finally said, "Okay."

Jesse rolled to his back bringing Abigail along until she straddled him. The majority of her lovely hair slid over one shoulder, but he could still see her nipple through the curtain of her locks and the seductive visual made a groan escape.

The silken feel of her thighs against his legs tested his ability to remain calm, cool and collected. He wanted to thrust his cock deeply inside her velvet flesh and never exit. Instead, he nudged his dick into the opening of her slick hot pussy. Gravity would put him exactly where he wanted to go. Jesse watched for her reaction.

The surprise on her face as his cock thrust deeper and deeper without either of them moving was priceless. She sat motionless with his cock embedded as deep as it would go. Her hands clutched his shoulders and her face registered a look like she was afraid to move.

He brushed her hair away from her face and gazed deeply into her eyes. "Are you okay?"

Abigail nodded, but didn't move any other part of her body.

"Do you hurt?" he asked.

She shook her head and sighed, but still didn't move.

Jesse nudged his hips upward and his cock went even deeper. Her eyes closed and a tiny smile played around her lips.

"That's very wonderful." Abigail's eyes popped open and focused her gaze on his. With an added gleam and she whispered, "What do you want me to do?"

"Ride me. Like a horse." He placed his hands at her hips and lifted her up off his cock and back down again.

Grinning as if she'd just learned a new and exciting game Abigail rode him. She was good at it, too. The next movement was all her own. She slammed down on him and he sucked in a deep breath of pure pleasure. Jesse slid his hands up her body until he could cup her breasts and tease her nipples. He licked his finger and circled one nipple as she rode him. Hard.

Abigail moaned above him as he played with her breasts. She'd developed her own back and forth motion that made his toes curl. He placed his hand between their joined bodies and flicked her clit until she shrieked. The tell-tale vise-tight clamp of her pussy muscles around his cock signaling her orgasm came in tandem with her scream of pleasure. Jesse lasted three more strokes before his own climax shot through the end of his dick like it had a rocket powered booster.

After only a couple more strokes, Abigail slumped on him her sweat-slicked breasts sliding across his chest. Their perspiration mingled from shoulders to knees. Jesse slipped his arms around her back and held her tight. He found he was suddenly loath to release her.

Surrounded by endless strands of strawberry blonde hair, Jesse squeezed Abigail once and whispered, "You're amazing."

She moaned and snuggled closer. Jesse had never had a more gratifying sexual experience than with his once formerly prim and proper little miss. A thought occurred to him that perhaps he was dreaming...or dead. Perhaps he'd never woken after being hit on the head in that Allied Supply Hut. If so, what a way to go. It was the last thought before he drifted into a long awaited sexually exhausted sleep.

* * * *

Abigail wanted to sing. She wanted to dance too, but she remained quiet. Jesse slept peacefully. No need to wake him and endure any embarrassment over the spectacular sex they'd shared. She extracted herself from his bed and his wonderful body slowly, so as not to wake him. She placed a tender kiss on his shoulder and he stirred so she backed away. Once she assured herself he was settled and still sleeping deeply she searched around the room to find all of her vast number of undergarments.

Dressing quietly, she pulled on her shift and the first two petticoats then brought the rest of her skirts out into the main part of his ship away from his peaceful sleeping form. Every swish of her skirts across the floor made such a racket, she knew he wouldn't sleep through it much longer. She closed the bedroom door quietly to finish dressing next to the cockpit of his aircraft.

Abigail knew what a cockpit was from the museum she'd gone to once. The mostly intact wreckage of the Outer-World space craft had been on display since her childhood. The Saints of Aria likely put it there for the male population as a warning of what "not" to get involved in. Women weren't usually allowed in such historically rich places, but her parents had been less rigid about her upbringing with regard to what women were "allowed" to do.

She glanced at the two chairs fastened permanently to the floor in Jesse's cockpit. The seats faced a board filled with various instrumentation situated beneath a narrow window currently closed off to the outside.

Memories of lovemaking with Jesse filled her with tingling warmth and desire as she shifted her final petticoat in place. She'd never forget the feeling of the exquisite release he brought within her body. He awoke a passion she never imagined herself capable of. She had screamed as the core-clenching sensation rushed through her body and the memory made her blush again.

Abigail carefully opened the bedroom door and peeked in on Jesse one last time. He continued to slumber peacefully in his bunk, his beautiful face relaxed. She vowed never to forget him or this wonderful afternoon. She closed the door again quietly before melancholy surrounded her heart.

Picking up the bulky accelerator module, and balancing it on one petticoat laden hip, she made her way out of Jesse's shuttle and headed back to town. She'd bring the part to Dooley so he could fix his dilapidated ship. Then they could continue their journey to Raylia and her next husband…her next life.

Heart heavy, and wishing for things that could not be, Abigail hitched the bulky metallic machine part higher on one hip and entered the sparsely populated area of Downtown Delocia Common. She walked slowly toward the end of the town's only dusty street headed for Dooley's ship. She kept Jesse's face in mind with each and every step toward a fate she wished weren't hers.

The vision of Jesse's satisfied smile would help when she gave over the part to Dooley. The reprobate captain would think she spread her legs for Horace. A wayward thought occurred. She hoped Horace wasn't angry that she'd gotten the part by sleeping with his employee. A sense of satisfaction at beating the system forced a smile to her lips. She quelled it and moved to the entry hatch of Dooley's ship.

Stepping into the dark slightly sour smelling space of the ship she traveled this far on, she wandered towards the sound of several raised voices coming from the communications room.

Abigail moved into the room where Dooley had told her to video-phone Horace at the Allied Supply Hut, and an event which ultimately changed her entire life, heart and soul. She hid another inappropriate smile and walked to the center of the men gathered all talking at once.

She noticed the law enforcement men first and stilled. Beyond the shoulder of the taller lawman, she observed a piece of her luggage opened on the table exposing her personal things to all assembled.

"What is going on here?" she demanded. Stomping forward to belatedly protect her things, she almost dropped the accelerator module in her fury over her privacy being violated.

"There she is," Dooley shouted. "She's the one who did it to get that part she's carrying."

A very large law enforcement official approached her. "Ma'am, where did you get the part you have there?"

Abigail looked down at the accelerator module and back up into his seemingly very suspicious eyes. "At the Allied Supply Hut."

"Do you have a receipt for your purchase? I need for you to show it to me."

Abigail felt the prickly warmth of embarrassment rise in her cheeks. She didn't have anything but a fond memory as receipt. "Not exactly."

"What exactly then, ma'am?"

"I traded something for it." Blistering heat rode over Abigail's face as the sexual memory seeped into her mind. "You can ask Mr. Horace's employee."

Dooley became animated, fairly dancing on the balls of his feet. "There! See? She's lying. Horace don't have nobody working for him. She did it."

"Did what?" Abigail asked as a layer of dread descended.

"You killed Horace." Dooley practically frothed at the mouth in accusation. "Shot him dead to get that part. Yes, she did."

"Do you have any other weapons on your person, ma'am?"

Abigail started to answer in the negative, but then remembered the crystalline handled gun ensconced in the folds of her petticoats.

The crowd parted in the room and she could see a large gun lying across her sleeping shifts in her bag. *Where did that beast of a weapon come from?*

"Ma'am?" The law enforcement official stood towering over her demanding an answer.

"I have a small gun."

The large lawman put a hand on his own weapon and asked, "Where is it, ma'am?"

"In the folds of my petticoats."

"I told you she was a blood thirsty one. Arrest her!"

"Shut up, Dooley," the law enforcement man threatened. He turned back. "I'm sorry, ma'am, but I'm forced to place you under arrest for the murder of Horace Buresh."

Chapter 6

Jesse woke suddenly and for a moment couldn't remember where he was. He shot up scrambling to the edge of the mattress then calmed down realizing he currently rested in his own damn bed.

Naked.

Across the room, he saw his clothes. Right where he'd shucked them off quickly to… "Abigail!" he called out stumbling from his bunk.

Jesse opened the bedroom door, but she was gone. He noticed she took the accelerator module. One hour's worth of feminine companionship had been paid after all. He shouldn't feel let down, but he did.

The lingering scent of fresh honeysuckle in the small space of his cockpit made his soul ache. He glanced at the fuel regulator for his own ship on the table and shook off his depressed thoughts. He had places to go and he was already late. He grabbed his pants off the floor, slipped them on quickly and took the fuel regulator to the engine room. He did his level best not to notice the musky delectable scent of her on his skin while he worked. An hour later he had a functioning engine and no reason to stay on Delocia any longer.

Jesse sat in his pilot seat pretending he couldn't see the rumpled sheets on his bed. The exquisite lovemaking with Abigail would forever be attached to that bed. He glanced at his bunk room out of the corner of his eye as a vivid memory of skin sliding against silken flesh permeated his mind. He sighed deeply. Why was he just sitting here? He needed to get out of here and yet an errant thought nagged at him. Freckles across a pert little nose bothered him, most likely.

No. Something else. *What am I forgetting?*

He shook his head, dismissed the bad feeling and finished his pre-flight check preparing for lift off. The new appropriated fuel regulator worked perfectly. Technically, he hadn't stolen the part. He left a small gemstone in place of the fuel regulator he'd taken deciding he didn't need any marks of thievery against his soul either.

Jesse leaned back in his chair, slid his gaze into his bunk room for one last reminiscence and noticed a dark tube about the size of a large gun barrel on the floor half beneath the bed. Jesse drifted into his room as Abigail's unique scent wafted around his head. He leaned over the bed and took a deep sniff. Damn. He missed her already.

Bending over, he retrieved what turned out to be a dark leather tube. It was slightly longer than the span of his hand measured fingertips to wrist. The length of the long edge was covered with a row of snaps. It was a small digital document protector with a broken outer chain attached at one end.

What the blazes is this?

Jesse opened the snaps along the edge and rolled out the blank proxy marriage document along with the dowry payment papers for one very prim and proper Miss Abigail Deveronne. She traveled on her way to get married to an unnamed man on Raylia according to these papers. Perhaps whatever man found the document protector underneath the miles of petticoats she wore.

Raylia. What a hell hole. Delocia was a garden paradise compared to the barren landscape of Raylia. Jesse swore an oath and closed his eyes. He shouldn't get involved. It wasn't any of his business. He closed up the document, rolling it carefully back into the protector, and snapped the leather cylinder shut. The document protector being the size, shape and color of a gun barrel made him pause. All of a sudden that elusive something he'd been trying to remember slid uncomfortably into the forefront of his mind.

The gun. The Allied Supply Hut. He'd almost been framed after being knocked unconscious. Then Abigail showed up.

Jesse swore another vile oath realizing he'd left the gun under the counter at the Allied Supply Hut still smeared with his DNA. Once those freckles had appeared, he'd completely forgotten about the gun and being framed for murder. He was a fool. A big, horny fool. He should pitch the cylinder into the trash, blast off this barren rock of planet as fast as possible and never look back. But then Abigail's awestruck expression during orgasm flashed in his mind.

Flipping the document holder between the fingers of each hand he thought about his options. Should he stay or should he go?

Abigail didn't intend to leave these valuable papers behind, had she? The broken chain told him it had been fastened somewhere to those endless petticoats. She surely didn't know it was missing. Also, it was a blank document. A single electronic signature made her someone's husband…even his signature would work. *No. Stop it. I don't need a wife.* Not even one with freckles and strawberry blonde hair all the way down to her luscious ass. He glanced back at the bed once in reverent memory of his hands attached to her silken derrière as she rode him.

Palming the document protector, Jesse pushed out a long breath and made his decision.

* * * *

Abigail was in trouble. Awful trouble. The kind of dilemma she didn't know how to get out of without an outsider's help. Unfortunately, none of the passengers on Dooley's ship had offered any assistance for her unearned plight. The others she'd traveled with turned away and avoided looking at her altogether almost the moment she'd arrived at the ship.

If she'd had anywhere to go, she might have run. But where could she go? Back to Jesse? No. At the time, she'd still believed he hadn't lied to her. Now, she knew differently.

Horace, the man she'd indirectly made a deal to trade parts for sex, had been murdered. He'd been murdered with a huge gun. The murder weapon had been found in her traveling bag on Dooley's ship. Added to this trouble was an unidentified witness claiming to have seen her pull the trigger after a heated argument over a machine part in the Supply Hut.

It was a lie, but she was a stranger on this planet and the witness was supposedly trustworthy.

She wanted to inform them that their trustworthy witness was a big fat liar, but instead she remained completely quiet. It was always better to remain silent for as long as possible in her experience. Nervousness often gave way to chattering. Talking too much would only land her in worst trouble.

During her arrest on Dooley's ship, the man tasked with bringing her to the jailhouse identified himself as Deputy Williams. He seemed like a decent enough man, but still, she hadn't replied to any of his or Sheriff Townsend's questions.

In fact, after Deputy Williams placed her under arrest, she hadn't uttered another word. He led Abigail to the Delocia jailhouse and placed her alone in one of the four bare cells until she decided to be more cooperative. The tall, handsome deputy also seemed very wary of Dooley, which was smart in her opinion. Dooley was a reprobate and a liar. Still, she didn't plan to cooperate or speak. She'd wait as long as possible and ponder silently what to do about her miserable future.

Aunt Eugenia was at the forefront of her mind throughout all this unfairness. Abigail would be terribly late getting to Raylia if she could manage to free herself from jail. In the meantime, she feared her aunt would suffer due to circumstances beyond her control.

She most assuredly hadn't said anything about Jesse. He'd been at the Supply Hut alone when she'd arrived. In listening to the deputy and sheriff talk about the case against her, she discovered Horace didn't have any assistants or part time people working for him.

Jesse had lied about working there. It begged the question of what *he'd* been doing there. He grabbed a machine part from the shelves before they exited the Supply Hut. He was her alibi, wasn't he? Or was he the murderer? If they found him and brought him here, would he also condemn her as all the others had?

Seated in this small jail cell and at the mercy of strangers, Abigail felt very alone in the universe.

Abigail made one decision as she sat quietly contemplating her life, she wasn't traveling with Dooley to Raylia. She'd find another way to get there. Another transport ship. What trade would be required for *that* journey since she didn't possess any funds? They'd taken the crystalline handled gun.

Jesse appeared in her thoughts again. If it turned out he wasn't a thief, or a murderer, would he escort her across the galaxy to her next husband? Did she want him to? It was a fanciful notion since she didn't even know him. Not really. Abigail shifted on the cot, tucking her legs underneath her, hugging her arms around herself, and spent the next few hours reliving her wonderful afternoon with Jesse.

Just when she was about to ask for a drink of water, Deputy Williams returned to her cell with a funny expression on his face.

"Why didn't you tell me?" His gruff, vague question alarmed her. She hadn't told him anything. What did he think he knew and why was he unlocking her cell door?

Abigail couldn't resist and spoke her first words since being arrested and put in this cell. "Tell you what?"

"That you were married. Your husband's here to collect you. Come on."

Abigail's eyes widened. *Was Myron back from the dead?*

Resisting the sincere urge to ask a bevy of questions, Abigail swallowed hard, held her tongue and followed Deputy Williams. She was led from the quiet cell to the outer jailhouse room. The man standing alone in the room had his back to her at first. With their approach, he swung around and a familiar warmth spread across her body.

Jesse.

"Hello, darlin'." Jesse approached her and placed a strong arm possessively around her shoulders, drawing her close to his side. She sagged in relief and wrapped her arms around his waist. Dressed dramatically different than the last time she'd seen him, his clothes were no longer raggedy or torn. She stared with question at his cleaned up appearance.

Jesse winked, promptly planted a quick kiss across her lips and said, "I was worried about you, darlin'. Came into town to see where you'd got to and heard at the tavern a strawberry blonde was in jail for murder of all the crazy things."

Abigail didn't say a word. Her throat muscles were clenched. Her first inclination was to bury her face in his chest, clutch him tighter and sob her gratitude, but he was lying. They weren't married and Jesse wasn't her husband. No matter how desperately she wished it were true.

"The murder took place this morning around ten give or take half an hour." Deputy Williams crossed his arms and widened his stance behind his desk. "Can you vouch for her whereabouts at that time, Mr. Pelland?"

"Yes, sir." Jesse grinned engagingly. "She was warming my bed about that time."

Abigail felt the flames of embarrassment shoot into her face like daggers. She wanted to deny it, but it was true. She loosened her hold from around his waist, but he wouldn't let her step away. The grip of his arm around her shoulders tightened and held her in place.

Deputy Williams cleared his throat and asked, "Can you prove you're her husband? I can't let her go on only your word, you understand."

Jesse smiled and nodded. He was lying…again. A thief and a liar. Why was she so attracted to him? He wasn't her husband and he would never be able to prove the deceit.

Keeping his arm firmly in place around her shoulders, Jesse pulled what looked like a proxy document holder out of his shirt pocket and handed it to Williams. A dull ache in the form of a very bad feeling centered in her stomach. *No. It couldn't be her proxy documentation.*

"This holds our marriage papers in the form of a signed proxy document."

Abigail, shook her head. *No. It couldn't be hers.* Stricken to have lost it and not even known it, she forcefully backed out of his arms and patted her petticoats in the place where the proxy document was supposed to be, but wasn't. Missing from her hiding place, she looked up in horror at the cylindrical object Jesse had just handed over to Deputy Williams. Her proxy documentation! Oh Saints above, had he signed it?

"Well, the signature is valid," Williams remarked and smiled at her shocked face. He glanced away and studied the document a moment before handing it back to Jesse. "Signed only today, though. Care to explain why her traveling bag was on a transport ship bound for Raylia?"

Jesse grinned. "Not unless I need to."

"You need to." Williams leaned two fists on his desk.

"The truth is I just came from Raylia. Dooley was bringing her to me, but I couldn't wait." Jesse winked at her and nodded at Williams. "So I came here knowing this is where he always stops for fuel and food replenishment."

"Convenient."

"And ultimately very satisfying." Jesse stepped close and tightened his arm around her once again. He was rescuing her. Even embarrassed at his explanation, she wanted to cling to him in gratitude. Flashes of their earlier tryst together invaded her mind. Her cheeks heated up yet again.

"Ever see this gun in her belongings?" Williams produced the large gun from a desk drawer letting it clunk onto his desk with a loud thud.

"That's a mighty big gun." Jesse leaned closer and looked at the weapon. "No sir, I can honestly say I've never seen this gun in her belongings. Is her DNA on it?"

"No DNA was found anywhere on it. Someone obviously wiped it clean. However, we have a witness claiming he saw Miss Deveronne—"

"That's Mrs. Pelland, if you don't mind."

Williams took a deep breath and released it slowly as if trying to temper an outburst. "Right. The witness claimed that 'Mrs. Pelland' argued with Horace over the price of a part and when he refused her offer, she raised the gun one-handed, took aim and pulled the trigger. Got him dead center in his forehead with a single shot."

Jesse snorted. "Darlin', do me a favor. Pick up that gun."

Abigail scrunched her brows together in utter confusion. Jesse nodded at her once, "Do it for me, darlin'."

Williams had a smug look on his face but only watched Jesse.

"Lift it." Jesse continued his staring contest with Williams. Neither of them watched her. What was the point?

Abigail took a single step. Her skirts swishing across the floor was the only noise in the room. She bent over the desk, wrapped her hand around the carved handle and tried to lift the pistol. It was much heavier than she expected. As she lifted it from the desk, the beast of a gun wobbled in her hand so much she almost dropped it.

She dragged it across William's desk, clutching it by the handle until she pulled it off the surface littered with paper. She almost dropped it on her foot until she steadied it with her other hand. Even holding it in both hands, they shook with the effort. She managed to lift it off the desk, but the weight of the big gun pulled her hands toward the floor. She struggled to keep it off the ground.

"She can put the gun down." Williams didn't glance at her. He continued to stare at Jesse. "Your point is taken. It was too heavy for her to lift using two hands let alone one. I already knew that."

Jesse smirked at Williams and grabbed the gun from her before she dropped it. He deposited the gun on the desk and asked, "Are you satisfied she's not your murderer?"

Williams narrowed his eyes at first into a stern look before a return smirk washed down his face. He took a deep breath and gave Abigail a piercing stare before turning back to Jesse. "She can go."

"Thanks." Jesse leaned down and kissed her lips quickly distracting her with the tingle of his seductive mouth.

Before Jesse reached for the door to exit, it burst open and Sheriff Townsend stormed in. Abigail hadn't seen him since she was taken into custody at Dooley's ship. She glanced down at the star pinned to the shirt on his chest. It was what she'd focused on as they arrested her.

Abigail flinched as Dooley's fat face appeared next in the doorway. He followed closely in the sheriff's wake. She grabbed Jesse's forearm to steady herself. He patted her hand and turned to face the new arrivals to the jail house.

"What's she doing out of her cell?" Sheriff Townsend demanded to know once he crossed the threshold and entered the jail's outer room. Abigail gripped Jesse tighter. The sheriff scanned her body in a familiar hungry fashion that made her very uncomfortable.

Williams answered, "This is her husband."

"No, it ain't!" Dooley's small black narrowly spaced eyes landed on her as if in disbelief. "She don't have a husband."

"I'm her husband. And I've already proven it." Jesse fixed a look on Dooley.

Williams stepped around the desk. "Her husband swears she was with him during the time of the murder."

"Well, a course he'd say that. Otherwise he'd get blamed." Dooley huffed.

Williams straightened his spine and put his hand on the butt of his gun. He asked, "Why would her husband get blamed?"

Sheriff Townsend turned to Dooley and shoved him against the wall. He pulled his gun from the holster on his hip and stuck it against Dooley's chest where his heart, if he had one, was located. "Shut up.

Don't say another word."

A split second later Williams pulled his gun and jabbed it into the Sheriff's back. Abigail clenched Jesse tighter.

"Drop your gun, Townsend." Williams said to the sheriff in a low cold tone.

"What's wrong with you, Williams? Take your fucking gun out of my back."

Deputy Williams narrowed his eyes and bent closer to Sheriff Townsend. "I know you think I'm stupid, but I recognized the gun you planted. You got it from that crazy bartender we apprehended last year."

The sheriff didn't move at first, but after a moment he seemed to melt. Townsend lowered his gun from Dooley's chest. Williams grabbed it and stuck it in the back of his belt.

"You can't prove anything." Townsend's snarl put Jesse on edge. Abigail felt his muscles stiffen as she clung to him.

"I was first on the scene at the Allied Supply Hut, Townsend. Just like you planned, but I had some inside information you were unaware of."

Townsend grated out under his breath, "Fucking liar."

"Old Horace always told anyone who would listen that he didn't have the money to put disks in his recorders, but *he* was the liar."

Williams reached over to the drawer and pulled a triangular recording cartridge out of the desk one handed. "I found an interesting video of you shooting Horace in the head. And you did it because you wanted to be the first to fuck the girl he and Dooley connived into going to the Allied Supply Hut so you all could rape her."

Dooley turned to run, but Jesse pulled his gun and aimed it at Dooley's head.

Abigail spoke suddenly, "Sending me to the Supply Hut was a trick?" She fixed her gaze on Dooley's stupid expression. "You tricked me in order to…to…violate me?"

Dooley shrugged and didn't bother to hide his smirk.

Jesse hugged her closer as a gesture of comfort. He also pondered the inevitable difficulty of hauling his Infiltrator weapon out of its hiding place to maim Dooley and the Sheriff as an act of vengeance on her behalf. He wouldn't do it, but thinking about was satisfying.

"I'm sorry, ma'am," Williams glanced at her a moment before turning back to Townsend. "Once I recognized the gun, I figured you couldn't have lifted the gun one-handed, let alone have shot it well enough to hit anything. I snagged the disk and watched it while you were in jail."

"Why did you keep me in the cell all this time if you knew I didn't murder him?"

"To keep you safe." He sighed. "I didn't know you had a husband who'd come looking for you. I knew you weren't safe on Dooley's ship or anywhere else in this city with the Sheriff loose. I kept you here to keep an eye on you."

Jesse's eyes widened. "Thanks, Williams. Can we go now?"

"Just as soon as I put these two in jail."

"Fine. I'll help you."

After they were locked up, Williams gathered her two traveling bags out of a closet in the hallway where the cells were located and handed them to Jesse.

At his frown, Williams said, "These are her things from Dooley's ship. I brought them along for evidence. Plus, a bag of things we confiscated from her during her arrest."

Jesse scrunched his eyebrows. "I thought you knew she was innocent all along."

He nodded. "That's true, but I had to get the Sheriff to believe I wasn't on to him. I volunteered to watch after the 'prisoner' while he went back to make sure there wasn't a tape in the recorder. I knew he wouldn't find one because I'd already pulled it."

"Thanks, Williams. I owe you one," Jesse said.

"Yes, you do. I saw the part on the tape where they tried to frame you." He winked and smiled.

Chapter 7

Jesse promptly led Abigail outside of the jail house. He carried her bags one-handed as they exited. "Come on, darlin'. Time for that honeymoon I promised you." He closed the door on the soon-to-be-Sheriff Williams' sternly amused face.

Abigail stopped moving before they took another step. "Where are we going?" Her voice sounded panicked and out of control, much like her reeling mind from the exciting events of the day.

Jesse nudged her forward again with his free hand. "My shuttle." She still refused to move. He carried her large bag in his other hand and had a second slung over his shoulder.

"I've been there." Warmth flooded her cheeks at the sultry memory. "It was very nice, but I need to get to Raylia. I'm already late."

"Is Raylia your home?" His hands burned blistering warmth through the fabric of her dress where he touched her arm and back. Her core moistened in readiness listening to his deep voice.

Abigail paused a moment before admitting, "It will be…once I get married again."

Jesse's stone-faced expression didn't tell her what was on his mind. His eyes traveled down her body slowly and back to her face. "So…you were on your way to get married, but decided to stop off on this back water planet to fuck a stranger in your spare time? Did you forget your needlepoint or something?"

"I…" She put her fingers up to her cheeks to cool her face.

"Not that I didn't enjoy it, mind you, but I don't understand why you did it. What were you after? I mean beyond the obvious sexual element."

Abigail whispered, "I wasn't after anything. I simply needed the part so that we could continue our journey to Raylia."

"What were you planning to do once you got to the Supply Hut? Would you have had sex with Horace?"

Heat blasted her face in embarrassment. "No. Of course not."

"How were you going to get the part?"

Abigail thought about the crystalline gun which was now in the bag of returned "evidence" Jesse carried and her initial plan to point it at Horace's head to get the part. It didn't seem prudent in light of recent circumstances to reveal that information. "Does it matter?"

Jesse's questioning expression relaxed and he shrugged. "I guess not."

Abigail looked into Jesse's face. "Those men tried to trick me and whether or not I'd agreed they would have done horrible things." She dropped her gaze to concentrate on his mouth and added, "But what's worse, now you think I'm a whore."

He removed his hand from her back and rubbed his eyes. "No, I don't." He expelled a long breath.

She gazed into his eyes to determine whether he told the truth. His opinion of her mattered more than she realized.

"Yes, you do." She turned away.

Jesse tipped her chin up to face him and shook his head. "I think you've always lived under very strict rules that I don't pretend to understand. You didn't have the experience to deal with those men. I don't judge you—"

"You *do* judge me," she accused cutting him off. She jerked her chin from his warm grasp. "But it doesn't matter. I need to get to Raylia."

He took a deep breath and let it out slowly. "Fine. I'll take you there after I run an errand."

"But—"

"Sorry, darlin'. But I insist. I promise I'll take you wherever you want to go, *after* I take care of some very important business of my own." He let out another deep breath as if in regret.

She glanced down and noticed he held the proxy holder in his talented fingertips. Her eyes widened in horror. She'd forgotten. She put a hand to her mouth to hold in the sob which escaped anyway.

"What's wrong now?"

"The proxy is signed. You signed it! Now I…" Abigail sobbed again and the rest of her words got lost in her shuddering tears.

"Don't cry. I'll take you back to your family and explain."

"All the way back to Segoha? That would take too long."

His eyes narrowed. "You're from Segoha?"

Abigail nodded and sobbed harder. "I'm ru…ruined," she stuttered. "I'll never make it to Raylia in time."

Jesse looked skyward and shook his head. He probably wished he'd never met her. "I'll take responsibility. I'll say I coerced you."

"Pitney, my guardian, will press charges if you admit to taking me by force. Even an outworlder would go to prison."

"Oh? And what happens if they find out you were willing and in fact instigated what happened between us?" he asked quietly.

* * * *

Jesse watched as Abigail cast her gaze to the ground between them and shuddered. A flush came over her face partially obscuring those sexy freckles. He wanted her so badly it was all he could do to keep his cock in his pants.

"What happens, Abigail?"

She shrugged and rubbed her hands down her arms obviously opting to remain quiet.

"Like I said before, I don't pretend to understand your Pilgrim religious sect, but I'm not about to let my wife suffer for something I enjoyed so much."

Her head snapped up. "I'm not your wife."

Jesse held up the proxy holder. "Yes, darlin', you are. For now at least. Come on now, let's go." He led Abigail toward his vehicle waiting down the street. He was married again, but didn't dwell on that slightly disturbing fact.

Abigail stopped walking suddenly and sniffed. "I can't go to Raylia without valid papers. And I'm late." He noticed tears streaming down her face.

Jesse hated dealing with weeping women. "What?"

She lowered her head, covered her eyes and sobbed out loud again. "I need to go to Raylia. There is a man waiting to marry me." She lowered her fingers and sniffed again. "Now, I don't have valid proxy papers."

"Does this mean the honeymoon's over?" Jesse placed an arm gently around her waist and led her down the street. She didn't resist this time, but her trembling body touched him.

"My aunt was depending on me," she murmured woefully.

"Aunt? What aunt?"

"Now she'll end up in the elder house." Another anguished sob escaped.

"What's an elder house?"

She straightened and glared at him before snapping, "It's a horrible place where the elderly people in my sect are sent if they don't have anywhere else to go." Tears glistened on her long eyelashes threatening to spill over and cover the freckles dusted across her pink cheeks. "Pitney threatened to send her there if I didn't make it to Raylia in a month. With useless proxy papers, I won't make it. My aunt will suffer because of what I've done."

"We'll discuss it when we get back to the shuttle." Jesse led her to his vehicle and she offered no further resistance. It was long past time to leave this barren backwater planet for good.

He tucked all those skirts into the passenger side of his vehicle for the second time today and quickly drove the rover toward his shuttle. It wasn't lost upon him that when they'd traveled together the first time he'd been totally clueless about what was going to happen. He couldn't get the vision of her silken legs wrapped around his naked hips out of his mind as they rode in silence.

Jesse swore he could smell her and the trouser fabric across his lap tightened. His cock lengthened even more as memories of their earlier encounter teased his mind.

It was also not lost upon him that they were, in fact, married now thanks to a certain signature on the proxy papers she'd carried. Perhaps he *would* indulge in a honeymoon. After the small taste of her earlier, he already craved more. Unfortunately, she likely wasn't interested.

Intimate passion to relieve the ache in his groin was *not* going to be part of his immediate future. Upset over her aunt including the details he didn't understand shaped her attitude. He refused to add a sexual element to her worries.

They arrived at his shuttle and Jesse secured the rover inside the bay before helping her out.

Her face pointed to the floor and she didn't look at him. She was probably still chapped that he couldn't leave immediately to head for Segoha. He'd make it right with her, but he had his own issues to deal with first. Not the least of which started with an expensive appointment to secure his freedom. Lola waited to rendezvous with him to receive the huge payment she'd extorted. For his part, he wanted an end to the unwanted business between them.

And he was also late.

Jesse guided Abigail out of the shuttle bay and into the main cabin. The door to his private quarters was open and showcased the unmade bed. If he were to stroll in there, he had no doubt he'd still be able to smell their earlier tryst on the rumpled sheets. A stab of desire poked him in the gut and sent a message to his randy cock.

The word honeymoon and all that it implied still bubbled into his brain and he couldn't get the vision of Abigail's naked body out of his head. That first time he'd seen her body was indelibly etched in his brain. A flash of Abigail willing and waiting for him on his bed saturated his mind. The vision taunted him and made other carnal thoughts seep in. They'd taken turns on top for their short hour together, but so many other untried sexual positions remained available.

"Abigail." The husky sound of passion was unmistakable. He wondered if she had any idea where his thoughts wandered to.

At the sound of her name she turned and fell to her knees before him. Her head bent as if in prayer and her hands locked together on her lap. He groaned as he realized if she lifted her head to look at him, it would line up perfectly with the unruly beast of a cock growing rapidly behind his zipper.

He swore again as his dick throbbed forward in anticipation of an imminent oral lesson.

"I'm so sorry." She sniffed once and he watched as a tear fell on the fabric of her dress.

"Sorry for what?"

Her face lifted. Jesse calmed his growing desire for her when he saw the distress etched in her features.

"I spoke sharply to you in public outside of the jailhouse. You saved my life, but I only thought of myself. Please. Will you forgive my shrewish words, my husband?" She lowered her face to her lap again and added, "I'll understand if a punishment is forthcoming." Her head remained bowed, her shoulders tensed as if she expected him to lash her.

"Stand up," he demanded.

Abigail's face lifted quickly to his as her spine straightened. His cock pulsed again but her tear-stained face tamped down his ardent libido. Jesse reached out a hand to her, grasped her extended arm at the wrist and pulled until she stood.

"If you learn nothing else about me, Abigail, please get this one thing straight." Her eyes widened and a frightened look registered. "I'm never going to treat you like they do. I'm never going to punish you for speaking your mind even if I don't agree with what you say. Do you get it? Do you understand my meaning?"

Her eyes promptly narrowed in confusion. She licked her lips nervously and the vision of her pink tongue on her lips undid him. He lowered his mouth to hers and kissed her hard. He thrust his tongue in her mouth to take, but she willingly offered her kiss. She moaned and melted forward against his chest.

Jesse wrapped his arms around her and planted his hands on her ass. The layers of her petticoats hid what he knew to be the finest derriere he'd ever had the pleasure of cupping in his fingers. He picked her up and walked her to the control board of the shuttle between the pilot and co-pilot seats. He placed her on the empty shelf between the two consoles and tightened his grip around her shoulders. He wanted to rip her clothes off, but practicality intruded. It would be too time consuming to remove all those petticoats by tearing them off of her. He loosened his grasp and slid a hand between them to caress one lovely breast.

She moaned in his mouth when his thumb flicked over the tip of one nipple and whatever rational intent to get off Delocia quickly evaporated. He wanted a honeymoon first. Just a little one.

He pulled his lips from hers. "I want you. Tell me you want me, too."

"I want you." Her soft whisper caressed his mouth.

"Are you telling me the truth, Abigail?"

"I am. There's never been anyone like you. I always want you." The heavy lidded aroused look in her eyes made his final decision easy.

Jesse kissed a path down her soft throat and across the thin fabric of her dress to the top of one breast. He kneeled on the floor and lifted her dress and grabbed the bulk of petticoats in his fists, pulling them down and out of his way until he glimpsed her silken legs. Looking down at him, she smiled, lifting one foot and then the other out of the bundle of material. He threw the mass of it over one shoulder and focused back on his uncovered treasure.

His fingertips brushed along her soft thighs, as he made his way upward to her wet pussy. He traced a path up to her damp lower lips. Her musky scent, combined with her sharp intake of breath when he reached her curls, nearly made him climax.

Jesse ducked his head under her skirt, lifted the material away from between her legs to rest against her waist and placed his mouth directly on her clitoris. He traced her slit with his tongue, tasting her creamy essence and swirling the tip around her clit.

Abigail gasped as he slid two fingers inside her silky drenched sheath as he licked her. Sucking her clit between his lips, her body shuddered against his mouth and he groaned in pleasure. Seconds later she screamed and bucked as she climaxed in his mouth. The pulse of her on his fingers made him want to bury his cock deeply as he lapped up the last of her creamy release.

Jesse rose and loosened his trousers as he ascended. Catching her eye, Abigail's lovely face expressed exactly the post climactic gratification he expected to see. He had his cock in hand ready to pierce her, but she slid off the edge of the control panel. Her hands went to his chest before she slipped her arms around his neck and hugged him, kissing a path along his jaw until she nipped his neck playfully with her teeth.

"You make me feel so wonderful," she whispered and clutched him tighter. She kissed his throat trailing wet kisses to his ear.

His knees buckled as her warm mouth surrounded the tip of his earlobe and sucked. He saw the pin which held her tight twist in place and pulled it out. Her light coppery locks fell around her shoulders and slid between them against his chest.

Jesse steadied himself with a hand on the upper corner of pilot's control panel and threaded her hair though this fingers to pull her back for another kiss. With the musky taste of her still on his tongue, he devoured her mouth in a decadent display. Twisting his tongue against hers in wild abandon, he soon pulled away to answer the rampant itch of his throbbing cock now bouncing in anticipation of imminent satisfaction.

The vision of her swollen moist mouth and adoring expression forced short breaths between his lips to garner some control. One hand was still fisted in her soft hair. He glanced down at the table behind her and quickly figured out the next sexual position he wanted to try.

"Turn around," he grunted.

She frowned slightly but obeyed his command. He temporarily released the hold on her hair until she turned and faced away. He placed a hand in the middle of her back and pushed her forward until her hands rested on the control panel. He lifted her skirts now sans the endless petticoats until he could see her bare ass. He shot his fingers through her hair and grabbed another handful, wrapping the strawberry tresses around his fist.

Grabbing his swollen ready-to-burst cock, he plunged deeply inside her pussy aiming for her womb. She moaned and her inner muscles clenched down hard on his dick in response to his eager penetration. She thrust her ass backwards until his cock lodged even deeper inside her body, the sensation of which made his eyes practically roll back in his head with pleasure.

Her whispered plea, "deeper, please," sent a pulse to his cock. Her hips thrust back banging her bare legs against his thighs and almost sent him to orgasmic bliss. He clamped his ardor tight.

Jesse shook with the need to release. He leaned down steadying a hand on the console and pumped his cock in and out of her tight, wet heat slowly. Rhythmically. Repeatedly. He fondled the soft strands of hair between his fingers. Rocking forward and back, in and out, he made love to her as it occurred to him that this was the pinnacle of his sexual experiences.

Abigail panted as he moved within her. When she arched her back and he felt her pussy clamp down again, he knew she'd climaxed. The ripple of her orgasm gripping his cock forced him to pause a moment.

One final deep thrust forced a growl from his lips as his orgasm spiraled through his needy body exploding through the end of his cock in blissful release. Spirits in heaven above, Abigail felt so good.

Glancing down at her hair in disarray with her skirt thrown up around her waist as he fucked her from behind heralded the best sex he'd ever experienced. That was his last coherent thought before collapsing forward. He slumped on top of her, one hand still caught in her hair, the other plastered to her smooth sexy ass. He trapped her against the command console until he could catch his breath and lift up without falling on the floor.

After a few moments, when the rushing noise in his ears settled down, he heard her harsh breathing. Good.

"Am I crushing you?" he murmured.

"No," came the muffled reply.

"Good. Because I can't move yet."

Her low sultry laughter tickled his satisfied libido to life again, but he didn't have time to spend the day with her like he wanted to. Perhaps once they were back on the *Dragonfly* and on a course to his distasteful rendezvous, they could partake of each other again.

Flipping up her skirt up to take her against the control panel of the shuttle was great, but he wanted her naked, sweaty and slithering over his body in his large bed on the cruiser. His ever ready cock bobbed within her body in approval of his plan.

He'd certainly never look at his shuttle instrument panel the same way again. He smiled and lifted off of her. His gratified cock slipped from her warm body hating to leave.

"I need to get back to my ship," he remarked, forcing his stiff joints to move as he pulled away from her sweet body. Abigail's skirt slipped back in to place albeit slightly rumpled as she pushed herself away from the console. Turning to face him, a blush crept over her face.

"I guess you aren't mad at me anymore," she said quietly.

He winked at her. "Never was."

"Good." She nodded. Her freckles always stood out more when she blushed. Jesse couldn't resist one more kiss. Leaning to within a breath away, she surprised him by closing the distance and connected with his mouth first. Her lips were soft and yielded to his when he licked them open slowly. Her hands pressed to his chest and his cock throbbed at her touch wanting her one more time.

He broke the sweet kiss, cleared his throat and said, "You can go get cleaned up in my private cabin. I believe you know where it is."

She smiled engagingly, nodded and moved away on slightly unsteady feet toward his shuttle bedroom scooping up the mass of petticoats on her way. Jesse fastened his pants and resisted the urge to follow her.

Instead he turned to the recently christened shuttle command console, slid into his chair and powered up the engines. He checked to make sure the fuel regulator he'd installed was working properly. Instrumentation was green across the board for an immediate takeoff and thankful that his less than soft landing on Delocia hadn't broken anything else.

Jesse shot his hand through his hair and stood up from the command console taking a deep breath. With it came the scent of their recent love-making. He couldn't wait to get back to the *Dragonfly*. "Abigail," he called turning toward his bedroom, "I'm preparing for take off. Are you ready?"

She appeared at his doorway. "Yes."

"Let's get you buckled in the co-pilot seat."

"I don't know how to operate a ship."

He laughed. "That's okay. You can just watch. It won't take us too long to get to my cruiser."

She bobbed her head once. "All right."

Jesse pushed the ship to ship communication button to call his engineer again. "Tiger? Come in, Tiger. This is Pelland."

After a lengthy pause, Tiger answered. "Glad to finally hear from you, Captain." His usually jovial tone was replaced by a surly one.

"What's up? Everything all right on the *Dragonfly*?"

Another pause. "More or less. Please tell me you're on your way back."

"Yep. I have a fresh fuel regulator installed and I'll be there shortly. Get everything powered up and ready to go. I'll want to leave as soon as the shuttle is secured inside the bay."

"Um…all right. We'll be ready to go."

"Is that message still waiting for me?"

"Yep. You want me to tell you—?"

"No. We can talk when I return." Jesse suspected the "message" was a scathing holographic one from Lola about the money she decided he owed her from the scam she'd pulled. The one he fell for hook, line and sinker. Damn it. He wasn't ready to deal with Lola just yet seeing as how he was still mid-honeymoon with his new and unexpected wife.

How had his life gotten so damn complicated?

* * * *

"Hold on," Jesse informed her as she gripped the arms of the co-pilot seat next to him. "The takeoff can be a little bumpy."

After experiencing all that she had today, Abigail decided she was ready for absolutely anything.

The flight to his cruiser, the *Dragonfly*, was a fairly smooth ride. Dooley's ship had sounded like it was going to fly apart into thousands of pieces when they'd taken off from her home planet of Segoha. The subsequent travel through space had been bumpy and fraught with dips and curves as if the steering was allowed a mind of its own with regard to direction.

Jesse didn't speak much on the short trip. He pushed buttons and occupied himself at his console. She didn't know how he was so calm, when she was so electrified by what had happened before take off.

Abigail sat quietly, but on the inside her body quivered with an unidentified need. She watched Jesse out of the corner of her eye as he flew the shuttle through space. She watched his hands, remembering how the rough texture of his fingers had caressed her so intimately. She closed her eyes and sighed in memory.

Jesse's voice calling his ship brought her out of her reverie. "I'm on approach, Tiger? Open the shuttle bay."

"Roger that, Captain. Welcome home. Really glad to see you."

"Aw shucks, Tiger, don't start crying."

Tiger responded tartly, "That message has become more urgent in your absence, Captain."

"Of that, I have no doubt. See you in a few." He flipped a button and the connection was broken.

Jesse turned to her for the first time since they'd blasted off Delocia. "Here it is. Home sweet home."

"It's a very big ship." Abigail hadn't ever spent much time around machinery or riding in mechanically run vehicles. She found it very exhilarating to fly through space. She'd miss it once she settled down on Raylia. The thought of saying good-bye to Jesse sent a stab of pain to her heart and forced her to blink back tears. She took a deep breath to calm down.

Jesse squinted "You okay?"

Abigail stared deeply into his eyes. "Do you promise to straighten things out with my guardian without telling him what intimate things I've…" she paused and flashed a quick glance, "done with you?"

His sensual bedroom eyes turned their entrancing gaze on her. "I promise. We'll leave for your home planet as soon as I take care of this urgent errand. I'm sorry for what I said to you outside the jail in Delocia. I didn't mean to make you cry."

She didn't quite understand, but nodded. The men from her planet never apologized for anything. He was technically her husband and according to the laws of her lifelong existence, she was required to obey him. Abigail wondered what it would be like to remain his wife until parted by death. Wake up, Abigail. He only married you to save your life. You don't get to keep him. *But I wish I could.*

The shuttle entered the bay of the largest ship she'd ever seen. Sleek and black, there were two rounded oval plates stacked off center from each other connected by another oval shaped tower and finally two cylindrical tubes attached horizontally to the lower oval plate. Once parked, they exited the hatch next to the rover vehicle to the metal floor of his large cruiser.

A small, wiry man with messy, short, dark hair and several days' growth of beard approached them quickly from another door.

"Good to see you, Captain." The man paused in his stride when he noticed her, but caught himself and kept moving until he stepped directly in front of them.

"Tiger, meet Abigail. Abigail, this is my engineer. We call him Tiger because no one can pronounce his real last name."

"Ma'am." Tiger nodded once politely, but she got the strong impression that he wanted to talk privately with Jesse.

Tiger leaned over and whispered something in his ear. She wasn't sure but thought Jesse went a little pale.

Jesse urgently whispered, "Where?" and Tiger motioned to the door he'd come through.

Turning to her quickly, Jesse patted her arm once. "I need to go deal with something very important. I'll be right back." He winked.

Abigail nodded politely. "I'll wait here."

The two men strode off out the door on the right side of the room whispering urgently between each other.

Abigail barely had time to look around the shuttle bay after they disappeared before another door across the room banged open. A tall strangely dressed woman stepped through the hatch and approached Abigail with strident steps and a face contorted in anger.

"Jesse Pelland," she screamed, "you better have what you owe me right now or you'll never get rid of me! I'll hound you until you die. I'll go all the way to Hell if I have to."

Abigail stared at her unblinking. Her eyes widened as she focused on the woman and her blatantly revealing clothes. She'd never seen an outfit such as the woman wore.

The frightening woman was very tall, perhaps because of her five inch high heeled footwear. She had long black hair swinging back and forth down her back. As she strode closer, Abigail noted the mass of dark locks were pulled into a large pony tail made up of several smaller braids. Bright colored beads of every color and threads to match were woven in to the braids of her hair undulated and made her head seem alive when she walked.

The black shiny clothing she almost wore barely covered her breasts and below her belt. Her black boots sported spiky stiletto heels. The soles must have been made of metal because they clacked loudly as she approached.

"Where is he?" she demanded stepping directly into Abigail's personal space. The woman's pointy boots disappeared under the edge of Abigail's skirts.

Abigail took a half a step backward. "Who?"

The woman sneered and crossed her arms. "My husband, Jesse. He better not be hiding. And if he sent you out to slow me down, Little Miss Princess Innocent, I have no problem tearing you apart one petticoat at a time until you cry and beg for mercy."

Abigail took a full step forward shaping her mouth into a sneer of her own and asked the evil woman, "You're married to Jesse?"

"Yeah, sweet cakes, I am, as if it's any of your fucking business. Who the hell are you?"

The sharp tug of jealousy around Abigail's heart nearly put her to her knees in despair, but she didn't want to appear weak in the eyes of this hateful woman. She let the anger and hurt of her jealousy grow into retribution.

Evil thoughts of depraved anger consumed Abigail. She leaned forward and spat out, "I'm Jesse's wife, too."

Chapter 8

Jesse left Abigail in the shuttle bay to address the serious problem of Lola being on board his cruiser and loose somewhere. The holographic message he expected turned out to be a personal visit from his soon-to-be-official-ex-wife. The scam artist.

Lola was about to receive a shitload of money so Jesse could get rid of her once and for all. After unsuccessfully ignoring her, then trying to trick her, he gave up and decided the least painful way to a more amiable future was to pay her off. Money was why she'd tricked him into marriage in the first place.

"Why didn't you warn me?" Jesse fairly snarled at Tiger on the way out of the shuttle bay.

"When she first got here, she wouldn't let me tell you. And the last time you called, *you* wouldn't let me."

"How could you leave her alone? She probably has every precious metal extracted from the waiting area."

"What precious metals?" Tiger huffed. "We don't have any in the waiting area. Besides, I only left her alone to come and *warn* you." His tone was indignant.

Jesse knew the disaster named Lola was a catastrophe of his own making. "It's not your fault. It's mine for getting into this mess."

"Sorry, Captain. I know she can't be trusted, but I didn't want you taken off guard by her screaming hissy fit immediately when you came on board. She's been following me better than my own shadow since she arrived and she's mean."

"Tell me about it. That woman could make a snake cry."

They rounded the corner to the very obviously empty waiting

area. Jesse raised both arms over his head imagining lots of bad things at Lola wandering freely through his ship. "Where is she?"

"Don't know. This is where I left her."

They turned at the sound of Lola's brash voice shouting from the shuttle bay they'd just left. Abigail. Lola. Same room. Damn it.

Jesse heard Lola's signature cackle laced with maniacal glee as he and Tiger ran hell bent for leather back to the shuttle bay. He entered in time to hear her say, "I don't believe you. Jesse would never marry a mouse like you after he's been with me." She arched an eyebrow up, leaned close to Abigail and licked her lips making a slurping noise.

With her arms crossed, not backing down a single inch, Abigail replied, "I don't have to parade around half naked to prove to the world that I'm not a mouse or that my husband desires me." She leaned closer and whispered something else to Lola that he didn't hear.

"Lola, what are you doing?" Jesse trotted closer. "Leave her be."

"Relax. Your new little mouse of a wife has a ferocious bite all her own. She wants to fight me for you." Lola cackled in glee again. "Should I do it, Jesse? Want to see me eat her for breakfast?"

Jesse gave Abigail a raised eyebrow stare of disbelief. A stubborn expression including a beautiful moue shaped her lips.

Tiger entered the room at a steady trot and almost ran into Jesse's back. Hopefully, he'd missed the information about Abigail being his new wife. His crew would give him such grief when they found he'd married again after boisterously and repeatedly condemning the practice for the last month due to his hateful union to Lola.

Abigail turned to glare at him as he approached. "You failed to mention you were married."

"I'm not married."

"Really? Then who is this?" She pointed at Lola.

"My *ex*-wife." Jesse turned from Abigail and grabbed Lola by her upper arm, partially covering her red snake tattoo, which wound around the bicep and over her shoulder and ended with a diamond shaped head and a forked tongue. "Come on. Let's conclude our business, Lola, and then you can leave. I'm unpleased you're here. I told you I'd meet you at your ship."

Lola slid a hand around his neck and pulled his face close as if she were about to kiss him and whispered, "But I didn't trust you, lover. I knew you'd try to cheat me again if I didn't come in person." Her bright red lips set to extended pout mode came within a breath of his.

"Did you want to spend a few hours in the VR cube with me to say goodbye nice and proper like? We could invite your new little mouse and scare the shit out of her with all sorts of sexual deviance. Wouldn't that be fun?" She laughed again and the noise of her voice grated on Jesse's raw nerves.

"Stop it, Lola."

Out of the corner of his eye he saw Abigail move toward them. She slid between them effectively separating them and pushed Lola backwards hard enough to make her stumble in her spiky heels.

"You little bitch," Lola shrieked, but remained an arm's distance from Abigail and glowered at them. Catching Jesse's eye she sneered. "He was mine before he was ever yours, princess. Does is make you insane wondering about all the sexual antics we performed together?"

"I don't care what he did before he met me. Why don't you focus on the fact that he's mine now, giving you zero claim? Keep your distance or you'll find out that mice have big razor sharp claws when I scratch your cold black heart out. If you even have one."

Jesse needed to diffuse this potential cat fight before feminine fur went flying. "Tiger, get Lola's payment. It's hidden in the shuttle. You know where."

"Roger that, Captain." Tiger moved away darting into the shuttle. The expression on his face told Jesse he was intrigued by the almost cat fight between the two women.

"You'd better have the papers ready, Lola, or you don't get a single credit."

"Of course I have them, lover." She reached long black and red painted fingernails into her snug black thigh boot and produced a long slender document protector. The shape of it was similar to Abigail's proxy holder, but longer and thinner.

Abigail's spine stiffened at the endearment "lover" and her mouth set to a firm angry frown. When Jesse put his hands on her shoulders, she snapped her posture even straighter. He guessed he was in the dog house for failing to mention his psychotic ex-wife. He'd have to make it up to her later.

What did a new temporary wife expect as compensation in return for an ill fated lie of omission regarding a former wife? The twisted thought made his head hurt. Besides, it wasn't like he and Abigail were planning a life together.

Tiger exited the shuttle with the payment and his thoughts centered on the current situation. He took it from Tiger, opened the bag for her to see the blood money he'd acquired for her using his "ultra secret" gun after swearing he never would.

Lola smiled and opened the document protector she'd held so he could see it was a valid annulment signed and documented "official" with a date from over a week ago. After the payment, it would release him of any marital obligation to her.

Finally. Blessedly. He was free from Lola.

However, because of fate and a faulty fuel regulator, he was now bound to Abigail until he could sever his second marriage in as many weeks. The mere thought of losing Abigail had a much different impact. She didn't make his gut roil with acid at the mere mention of her name.

Lola took her bag of gems and smiled. "Did you want have one last fuck for the road, Jesse? We could have a threesome. The little mouse might be interesting as a frigid bedmate between us."

"Get out. You have your payment." Jesse didn't look at Abigail, but suspected her freckles were flashing neon around pink cheeks. "One other thing, Lola. If you ever see me coming, stay out of my way."

"Of course, lover." Lola glanced down into the bag of the purest crystal gems the Ksanthral system had to offer. It was the original bag he'd had thrown at him on a desolate asteroid in the upper atmosphere of Raylia's outer space field. He hated Lola for giving him no option but taking up his former GG Infiltrator revolver after swearing he'd never touch it unless it had to do with disarming someone holding the same "outlawed" gun. There was a reason he'd kept his illegal weapon and given up his precious pension and not for this nasty business enforced on him by Lola. *Damn bitch.*

"Our business is concluded. I want you gone. Don't come back." Jesse hoped she choked on the gems he'd procured to get out from under her spiky piercing heel. "Tiger?"

"Captain?"

"Escort Lola to her ship."

"Not necessary, lover, I know where my ship is. I'll be on my way." Lola winked at him and stormed out of the room like a vision from Hades, the metal of her thigh boots clacking all the way down the hall after she was long out of sight.

"Prepare for travel out of this quadrant. Have Pru get us on a course to Segoha."

Tiger froze for a moment before becoming animated regarding his travel plans. "Segoha? The Puritan planet? Why are we going there for gosh sakes?"

Jesse glanced at Abigail and back at Tiger willing him to figure it out or shut up.

"Oh. I'm sorry, ma'am. The excitement of Jesse's wife—"

"Ex-wife!" Jesse interrupted.

"Right, ex-wife. Well, it's rattled my brain. We'd be happy to escort a new passenger to Segoha."

Abigail flashed Jesse a disappointed gaze. He guessed she wanted to be acknowledged as his new wife. Seeing as how Lola was such a bitch about it. Shit.

"Actually, Tiger…Abigail is…well…" Jesse, loathed admitting

their relationship. His crew would chortle their collective asses off when they found out.

Abigail lifted worried eyes to his so he finished his sentence at the risk of being a laughingstock to his crew. "...she's my new wife."

"New wife? But you said it would be a cold day in Hades—"

"I know what I said. These are special circumstances."

Tiger laughed out loud thinking he joked. Turning his amused face to Abigail's perturbed one made him clamp down on his boisterous humor, but he still smiled.

"She's really my wife, Tiger. Get a hold of yourself."

Tiger nodded as his eyes watered in exuberant stifled laughter. "I'll inform the crew that we have a new destination." He turned and exited the bay chucking under his breath. Jesse had no doubt he couldn't wait to inform the crew of the *Dragonfly* about his new marital status as well.

Jesse took Abigail's hand and led her to his quarters managing to avoid anyone else. Abigail didn't resist. She seemed slightly dazed. Her glazed over shocked expression worked in his favor to deliver her to a more private place.

He opened the door to his quarters and pulled her inside. As soon as the door was closed she spoke. "Is the proxy paper you signed to marry me even valid?" Abigail whirled around in and angry huff.

"Yes. My fake marriage to Lola was annulled a week ago, but she wouldn't give over my copy of the official papers until I gave her half the value of my transport business."

Her eyes filled with tears. "Well, you must have thought she was worth it. Is that the kind of woman you prefer?"

"Not even close. I had to act fast before she opened any new expensive accounts in the name of Mrs. Jesse Pelland."

Abigail put her face in her hands and wept.

"She didn't mean one single thing to me." He moved close to comfort her, but she tore away from him when he placed his arms loosely around her shoulders. "Please don't cry, darlin'."

"Don't call me that, I'm shamed."

"What? Why are you shamed? I was the idiot who married that viper by accident."

"But she's so exotic. How can you even look at ordinary unimportant me? I'll never, ever look like her."

"I don't want you to look like her. I swear you're beautiful just as you are. You have the most adorable and irresistible freckles I've ever seen. I'm smitten."

"I don't believe you." She shook her head and snorted. "I know what I look like. My dress is ugly and outdated. Besides I'd never be able to wear such scandalous clothing in public, just as I know it's the type of garb men naturally desire."

"Not me."

She flashed him a harsh look. "I'm not stupid. And I don't believe you. After sleeping with the two of us…comparing us…" She trailed off and started sobbing again.

Jesse approached her and placed his arms around her. She didn't stiffen this time. "I never slept with her, darlin'. I promise."

Her head shot up in obvious surprise. "You didn't? Why not?"

"That's a long story best left alone to my foolish past."

She turned in his arms. Her anguish expression gave him pause. "Tell me, please." Her tear-stained face begged to be kissed. All those freckles dusted across her nose and cheeks made the blood in his veins come to life with rampant desire. He wanted her again.

Instead of seducing her right away, Jesse confessed the stupidity of the last month of his life and subsequent marriage to a gold digging whore.

"I landed on a planet I'd heard had lots of transport business. My limited research told me I'd discovered a veritable gold mine simply waiting for me to arrive to make money. So, I eagerly stumbled into the local celebration the town hosted to make as many acquaintances as I could. I figured I'd mix in and find all the rich merchants looking for a permanent transport ship to carry their goods across the galaxy. I saw visions of prosperous cargo flights and more business than I could handle dancing before my eyes. And I was stupid."

"It doesn't sound like you were stupid," Abigail remarked quietly. "So far it sounds very reasonable."

He grinned at her. "Well the stupid part came when I drank the local ale. A big mistake. I think I was intoxicated by the second mug. I laughed with the people of the town like I was their new best friend. An even bigger mistake. Then some loud music started playing and a whole bunch of women sauntered out of a nearby tent to dance. I thought they were the celebration entertainment. One by one each of the women approached and selected men to join them for a dance around the bonfire erected in the center of the town square and blazing into the night."

"Did Lola choose you?"

Jesse nodded. "Yep. Lola approached me to dance. I was so drunk by then I could barely walk. I declined at first, but she was insistent. I didn't want to piss anybody off, so we danced around the triangular bonfire. Once back at my original spot, she gave me another beverage before I could sit and led me staggering around the fire one more."

Abigail tilted her head. "And you weren't suspicious of what she was doing?"

Jesse shrugged. "I was too wasted. I didn't understand the significance of dancing around the bonfire and she didn't stick around to explain. The truth is, she promptly disappeared about then and I barely made it back to my ship without killing myself."

"What was the importance of the dance?"

"Unfortunately, twice around the bonfire on the first new moon of the third solar month with the same woman meant we were married according the local dictates.

"I didn't find this critical information out until the next day recovering from a monumental hangover in my bed. Lola came to the *Dragonfly* with a contingent of local officials weeping and wailing about my abandonment of her after the supposed 'ceremony' we'd participated in. The local officials called me names I didn't even understand and ordered me to live up to my obligations and care for her for face jail. I barely remembered her from the night before. I certainly didn't care for her."

"And the obligations were what?"

"Brides share equally in their husband's financial affairs. Most newcomers are advised of this, but because I couldn't be bothered before the celebration, I was screwed. It was my own damn fault for being is such a hurry to make money. Ultimately, I was forced to disclose the value of my transport business.

"Once we were alone, she told me she'd get an official Ksanthral system annulment and leave my life if I gave her one half the value of my business. So I did. You witnessed the pay off."

"You never loved her?"

He frowned. "No. I never had sex with her either."

A sudden smile lit her face. "Really? Do you promise?"

"Yep."

"And the proxy document you signed for me—"

"Is completely legal because my annulment predates it."

She considered things a minute before nodding. "Good."

"Now that I've taken care of my urgent business we can head for Segoha immediately."

"Thank you for telling me."

He gazed into her eyes "I'm sorry I made you cry."

"I'm sorry for displaying such a shrewish behavior towards that woman in public."

He shrugged. "Lola definitely had it coming."

Abigail's subsequent smile made Jesse glance over at his large comfortable bed. He wondered what his chances were of convincing her to share it. His cock throbbed with the desire for wickedly sensual acts and the memory of how comfortable his very large bed was.

"You can demand that I get in bed with you." Abigail uttered in a low husky passion-filled voice.

Jesse caught her gaze with his intense one. He leaned closer to her face and whispered against her lips. "I don't want to demand anything from you, Abigail. I want you to come to me willingly."

She licked her lips almost touching his as if considering his statement. "I shouldn't since..." She turned and glanced at the bed quickly. "...this marriage is, in fact, temporary."

"But you want to." Jesse stepped even closer and kissed one cheek. The edge of his lips touched the side of her mouth. His hands slipped to her shoulders prepared to do his utmost to convince her they were man and wife and could do anything they wanted to. *Legally*.

"Once we get to Segoha, I'll have to assure my guardian we didn't do all the things we've already done. I'm a terrible liar. One look at my blushing face and stuttering explanation and Pitney will know we've been intimate just by the way I gaze at you." Her bright pink face beseeched him to persuade her.

Jesse paused a moment in thought then said, "Correct me if I'm wrong, but as your legal husband on Segoha, and in front of anyone associated with the Saints of Aria, don't I speak for you?"

Abigail turned to him with an engaging smile and relief in her tone. "Yes. That *is* true."

"You don't have to talk to anyone. I'll speak to your guardian and anyone else we encounter. I'll even demand that you remain silent." He smiled. "I'll tell him Dooley gambled you away in a game of chance and we married in name only, so I could get your dowry. It's simple and best of all it's plausible."

She sighed as if suddenly indignant and said in a weary voice, "Plausible or not, it's still a falsehood."

"If we don't tell him the truth about what's happened between us, Abigail, a falsehood is all that's left to choose. That is unless both of us remain completely silent. That won't get the point across either." He raised his eyebrows to punctuate his point. "Can you picture it? The two of us and your guardian locked in an endless glaring contest."

She smiled and shyly looked away. "Perhaps."

"Tell you what," he added. "I'll demand more dowry money from your guardian and volunteer to take you to Raylia. That will make the negotiation more believable, okay?"

Jesse watched her wrestle with her conscience. Her brows furrowed in concentrated serious thought. While she pondered their future, he moved closer. She didn't stop him. He reached up to the bodice of her gown and started unbuttoning it.

"What…what are you doing?"

"Keeping myself occupied while you think. You look very uncomfortable in all these petticoats. Why don't I unwind you a little?"

"Unwind me?"

"Yes. Unwind means relax. If you want, I could find something else for you to wear while we're aboard my ship. My pilot, Pru, is about your size. She'd loan you something if you'd like to try slacks and a shirt."

Abigail blanched. "You wish me to wear different clothes."

"No. I only want you to be comfortable. The bottom hem of your skirt is about ten feet across in diameter with all those petticoats. I might have to widen the halls in my ship so you can walk around."

"Really? You're going to alter your ship?"

"No. Not really." He kissed her forehead. "I'm just kidding."

His knuckles brushed against her nipple straining against the fabric of her dress. He allowed his fingertips to purposely brush over her breasts. "But I'm not kidding about my desire for you."

Her sharp inhalation and the feel of her firmed nipples through her under garments made his cock harden. He knew it'd take at least two weeks to get to her home planet even going at top speed through worm holes and spatial tunnels. Two weeks to explore every inch of her lovely body before he had to give her up. Two weeks to try and get enough of her to last him forever once she was out of his life. It

Rogue's Run 93

didn't seem like nearly enough time to accomplish lifelong memories.

Jesse wondered if he'd ever think about Abigail without his cock coming to full attention. Her shy blush over everything touched him. Her sexy freckles called to him. So did the fragrance of her hair. So did everything about her.

He'd loosened all the buttons down to her waist before she grabbed his face with her hands and planted a ferocious kiss on his mouth.

Abigail released his lips only long enough for him to pull her dress down off her shoulders. She helped push it, along with her voluminous petticoats, to the floor. She stepped out of the pile of fabric and launched her body against his clad only in a thin under dress. Her mouth connected to his again. She did seem to love kissing.

The sexy mewling noises coming from her throat put his erection at about titanium grade tensile strength. He wanted to bury his cock inside her and live there.

The memory of her vise-tight pussy pulsing in climax against his cock as he thrust in and out holding her pinned to his command console in the shuttle, registered in his brain with primal gusto. He marveled, because it had only been a few hours ago. He didn't often spend more than one interlude per woman. He'd been so focused on his business that he didn't take time to enjoy the pleasures of the flesh beyond time in the Virtual Reality Room of his ship. There he chose any number of women, but never the same one twice.

Abigail was the only woman in years to share his bed more than once.

Jesse pulled her along to his large bed. He sat down on the edge wedging her between his legs. He stroked his hands across her body then pulled the under blouse she wore down her shoulders to reveal her pert, lovely breasts. His mouth found a rosy tip to suckle. The moan she released wrapped around his libido as he licked her nipple. He clamped it between his lips and sucked hard to her vocal pleasure. Her hands threaded through his hair as he kissed a path to her other breast. His mouth fastened around the hardened tip and feasted.

Abigail held his head closer moaning as he nipped and sucked. She broke from him panting and slid the thin shift off, kicking it aside. Jesse stood up and released his hands from her flesh to pull his shirt off. He wanted to be skin to skin as they had been on the shuttle that first time. He loosened his pants watching her blush from head to toe standing naked and trembling before him.

Undressing quickly, he wrapped arms around her soft warm body and kissed her mouth tenderly. Her arms draped around his neck. Her lovely breasts burrowed into his chest.

Jesse clenched her tighter and turned with her plastered to his body so he could place her in bed. He followed her down, sliding his body over hers slowly. Once covering her completely, he rested atop her soft form taking in the pleasure of the sexy skin to skin connection. She was so beautiful and so responsive to every caress, every kiss he placed.

Her lips kissed a path to his neck as he slid a hand between her legs to assess her readiness. Sliding two fingers between her lower lips, he sucked in a sharp breath as visceral images of them writhing together on the bed slipped into his mind. She was wet, warm and ready. He bathed his fingers in the moisture of her arousal and stroked her clit. She arched her back and moaned, clenching him closer. He lowered his head to suck at one nipple and then the other, rubbing her clit until he felt her curve in his arms in climax whispering his name on a satisfied sigh.

Jesse lifted his hips and moved so his dick brushed against her core inserting himself inside an inch or so. The pure shock of hot pleasure wrapping around his cock at entering her tight slick body forced the air out of his lungs.

"You feel so incredible, Abigail." Jesse impaled her slowly and deliberately then pulled out again as slowly as he'd entered. "I may never get enough of you." His whisper was lost in the wickedly sensual delight of stroking deeply inside her sweat slicked very aroused core. In and out. In and out he stroked with infinite tenderness. He wanted to release the orgasm he was on the verge of and yet hated to end the gratifying sensation he bathed in. If this blissful feeling went on forever, he wouldn't mind. Abigail touched his soul. Some part of him realized that he'd never get enough of her in a mere two weeks.

He'd need longer. Much longer.

Jesse reached between them to stroke her clit as he maintained the steady thrusts into her body. His mouth found her breast to suckle a nipple as she writhed beneath him. The tenderness of their slow lovemaking made him feel inebriated. Jesse's senses were on sexual overload. Abigail's hips jerked as she cried out and the telltale rhythmic pulse of her orgasm clenched his cock in its seductive grasp.

Inhaling deeply the flowery fragrance of her hair with the underlying scent of honeysuckle from her skin ultimately sent him into the throes of a powerful orgasm. Her arms circled his neck clenching him close once he collapsed against her.

Utterly spent.

Utterly delighted.

And utterly infatuated with his "new" and very unexpected wife.

Chapter 9

Leaving Abigail in his bed fast asleep, Jesse shook off his sated and satisfied post sexual glow to go explain another wife to his crew. Normally he'd tell them to go to hell, and do whatever he wanted, but he needed their help getting across the galaxy. He'd require further assistance once they arrived at Abigail's planet.

Segoha. What a dismal sanctimonious hellhole it had turned out to be the last time he'd been there. Poor Abigail. If he accomplished nothing else, he'd ensure she got away from there permanently and off to Raylia, if that's what she wanted. Although, at the moment, the thought of being separated from her made his gut clench.

Jesse didn't want her to find another husband, did he?

On the other hand, he didn't want another wife, did he?

Turning his thoughts away from indecisive stupidity, Jesse made his way to *Dragonfly*'s common room. The central location in the heart of the ship's titanium walls was a calming sanctuary when his life was in an uproar.

The crew shared their meals here along with meetings and training. Basically they shared life on this transport ship where he'd invested everything to improve the circumstances of his existence. He was fortunate having managed to recruit a crew that, for the most part, got along. An eclectic bunch, the disparity of their past served to bind them to a mission of cohesive livelihood. He trusted them. They were the only family he had.

Until Abigail.

Jesse closed his eyes and sighed. His strawberry blonde lover, presently slumbering in the recently rumpled sheets of his large bed, would not leave his mind for very long. He'd have a stern lecture with his libido later. For now, he needed to ask his crew for help and support on the unanticipated journey to a planet he'd relentlessly sworn to avoid.

Jesse strolled into the common room to find his entire crew waiting. He still didn't look forward to explaining about Abigail or Segoha. When they all broke into laughter over his discomfiture he knew the jig was up.

"Tiger informs us there is a brand new Mrs. Pelland on board," his shy pilot, Pru, remarked with a small grin shaping her lips. She was tall, lean and muscular with chin-length straight blonde hair framing her pretty face.

Jesse grinned back and decided Tiger spilling the news was a relief.

"Yep." Jesse nodded. "It's true. I got married again, shockingly enough."

Pru leveled a stare at him. "I heard tell she's the very opposite of Lola."

Jesse huffed, "You got that right. Abigail is quiet."

"Well, any wife of yours is sure to be entertaining," Tarik, his weapons officer, grunted. At nearly seven feet tall with genetically enhanced, and very visible musculature, Tarik made all those who dealt with him very nervous. Jesse felt it was his primary job to make others nervous.

It would be a triumphant return to visit Segoha with Tarik standing behind him when they went to speak to Abigail's guardian. Mentally, Jesse rubbed his hands together in glee at the prospect.

"She isn't here for long." Jesse crossed his arms over his chest. "I promised to take her home."

All the members of his crew smiled again.

Tarik made a tsk tsk noise. "You must be doing something wrong if she already wants to run home to her mama."

Jesse rolled his eyes and tried to explain. "Abigail was on her way to Raylia and an arranged marriage with proxy papers and a generous dowry receipt. I signed the papers to keep her out of jail and a murder they tried to frame her for."

The crew gave him varying dubious expressions regarding the tidbit of information about Abigail being framed for murder.

"She didn't do it," he said earnestly. More snickering followed. "They tried to frame *me* for the same murder until I disappeared with her."

His crew smiled at his expense and shared knowing looks with amused traded glances yet again.

"So, how much is the dowry receipt for?" Della asked. Tiny, with dark hair and sharp intelligent blue eyes, she was Jesse's communications officer and the smartest person he'd ever met.

"It's enough to make it worth our while to go to her home planet and collect it."

Della could do complicated mathematical equations in her head and pop out the answer almost as fast as the on-board computer. Plus, she had a vast working knowledge of legal contracts and the inherent loopholes therein, which he took advantage of regularly.

Tiger shifted in his chair and crossed one leg over the other. "And the fact that she's absolutely gorgeous had nothing to do with your sudden decision to sacrifice your life for her?"

Jesse narrowed his eyes and huffed. "I simply knew she didn't commit the murder she was accused of. That's it. No hidden agenda."

"Except for the unexpected trip to her home planet," Tarik said with a grin. "Followed by another lengthy journey to the other side of the galaxy and Raylia, also known as the fetid armpit of the Ksanthral system."

"That wasn't her fault," Jesse argued.

Tarik crossed his arms. "It also wasn't your problem, or ours, until you married her."

Jesse raised his gaze to the ceiling. "Fetid armpit or not, going to Raylia isn't a problem, is it?"

Pru shrugged and replied, "I guess not. The only thing I know about Raylia is that it harbors a small cult of the Saints of Aria. They have a settlement just outside of town. They've spent centuries trying to tame the wild outlanders there who most likely laugh at their efforts at repression."

The fact that Pru was so vocal today about this subject surprised Jesse. He knew she shared his opinions regarding the people living on Segoha, but she absolutely never commented on it out loud.

"The folks on Raylia are probably less obsessive." Jesse scoffed.

"No. The truly fanatical religious zealots live on Raylia." Pru laughed without a shred of humor in her tone. "They try valiantly to bring religion to the wicked heathens there." She closed her eyes, shook her head and took a deep breath as if trying to expel a bad memory.

Jesse decided it was time to confess. "Speaking of fanatical religious zealots and wicked heathens is a good segue for my next announcement."

He paused before mentioning the next shocker. They would get a hearty laugh out of it. The expectant faces of his crew turned toward him to hear where they were going next and the destination of Abigail's home. They were all aware of his first escapade to Segoha. They knew he had a bad taste in his mouth from the last experience.

"Our new destination will truly surprise everyone. I find it difficult to believe it myself, but I've promised Abigail and the truth is I think a little vengeful payback is in order."

Pru spoke. "You know what they say, 'revenge is a dish best served cold.' Are we going someplace with freezing glaciers and frigid climate?"

"Nope." Jesse pictured his singular voyage to Segoha. The surface of the planet was mostly dry plains like every other dusty planet in this system. There were pockets of water on the planet, but most in the galaxy didn't know it. He'd dealt with The Saints of Aria on Segoha only once, however, it was well before he'd assembled his current crew.

After spending only half a day there, Jesse had left the sanctimonious leaders in a quiet rage. He'd been summoned by them for what they called a bounteous transport business opportunity. Back then it had been a chance he'd desperately needed due to his miserable finances after starting his transport business.

Once on Segoha, Jesse had been smugly lectured on his lifestyle choices and after a couple of hours it became clear they weren't going to offer him any business opportunities, lucrative or otherwise. He also wasn't the first to fall for their come-on which was of little comfort. The Saints of Aria merely wanted to belittle him. They had tricked him and he'd fallen for it.

The trip to Segoha had been a monumental waste of time and worse, he'd used up precious resources to go there. He'd stormed back to *Dragonfly*, left in the custody of his short-term crew. They were a for-hire group and he hadn't entirely trusted them. He'd made course for Chronos because although the jobs there were usually unsavory, he needed to pay his bloodthirsty temporary crew. Once on Chronos they'd abandoned him anyway, because of the farce visit to Segoha, the bastards. But not before beating him bloody for their trouble. He was lucky to have survived them.

He'd discovered his pilot, Pru, on Chronos. Or actually, she'd found him bleeding and cursing his life in a crumpled heap behind his ship. She wandered to where he was and sat watching as if wondering if he'd make it. He wondered the same. She brought him water and helped him stand.

Jesse shared his last rations with her and later the same week he found her wandering around behind his ship where they'd first met. While interviewing for new crew members, she hung around as he acquired a new crew. Skittish and hungry, she'd signed on with him quickly as if looking over her shoulder the entire time.

Pru was the best pilot he'd ever had to pleasure to fly with. She had a natural talent for it that he knew in his gut wasn't learned in simulators or books. He didn't even know where she'd trained as she never spoke about her past.

Jesse didn't care. He'd assembled the rest of the crew over the next couple of months. With every interview, she'd been jumpy and nervous her eyes continually darting to the floor as they spoke with candidates.

At the time, Jesse thought perhaps she'd been abused in some way and vowed to never let another man worry her. He'd hired Tarik as his weapons officer, in part, to ensure the customers he flew for never bothered his female crew.

Tarik was his final acquisition. Chosen primarily because Pru was so fascinated with him, and had been from the first time she laid eyes on the warrior. She was never frightened of Tarik, even as big and scary as he looked. Tarik was the first man Jesse had ever seen Pru actively stare at instead of the floor during an interview. He was the only one she'd spoken to out of the seemingly hundreds he'd interviewed.

Ultimately, Pru's enthrallment with Tarik and lack of fear of him helped Jesse make his choice.

"So tell us, Jesse, where does the new Mrs. Pelland hail from?" Della asked.

Before Jesse could answer, Tiger piped up. "Get this. The new *quiet* wife is getting Jesse to go back to Segoha." Tiger laughed out loud as did Della.

Jesse noticed immediately that Pru and Tarik did not find the destination amusing. Pru turned to him with wide eyed shock on her face. Tarik looked like he wanted to kill something.

Having sworn repeatedly to his crew that he wouldn't ever grace the planet Segoha's atmosphere again, Jesse had also sworn he wouldn't ever get married again. Fate was having a great time screwing over his vocal absolutes and then laughing at his expense.

"I know it's crazy, but it's true. I promised Abigail I'd take her back to Segoha. It's where she's from. However, I promise we won't be there long."

His announcement was met with silence from half the members of his crew, but he plowed forward anyway. "So Pru, I want you to plot the fastest course to Segoha—"

Pru blanched and stiffened even as her head started shaking back and forth indicating a negative response to his request.

Jesse scrunched his eyes with lack of understanding.

Seated behind Pru, Tarik stood and crossed his arms. Palpable anger came from him in waves before his thunderously ominous voice announced, "No. We'll follow you anywhere else, Captain, but not there."

Jesse didn't believe he'd heard correctly. Was this another joke? He took a deep breath to control a sudden anger and let the air out of his lungs slowly out to summon calmness. "Care to explain why not?"

Tarik and Pru exchanged a look, but Tarik was the one who answered with an unequivocal, "No!"

"What the hell?" Jesse threw his hands in the air. "Could one frickin' thing go right today?"

Reigning in his ire over his mutinous crew he continued in a calm voice. "Let me explain. I need to go to Segoha because I promised Abigail and I obviously can't go by myself. So if you could please explain to me why my crew is about to mutiny, I'd be much obliged."

Pru gave Jesse a watery smile as Tarik uncrossed his arms and laid one protectively across her shoulders. Jesse stared in fascination at his weapons officer's tender gesture. The two of them had *never* displayed any public affection on the ship, or anywhere for that matter.

Whatever went on between them in private, whether sexual or completely platonic, hadn't mattered. They did their jobs well and he sensed in Pru a quiet rejuvenation of spirit so different and so much better from the first time he'd met her. Jesse didn't ask either of them because it was none of his business, but he suspected a personal relationship existed.

A few weeks after hiring Tarik and during a standoff with several angry miners over rations, water and money, Tarik stepped in front of a laser blast meant for Pru during the negotiations.

The blast would have killed her. Tarik was down for a few days as his implanted nano-technology repaired the blasted tissue. Jesse didn't question Tarik's motives regarding Pru after the incident. Knowing Tarik would lay down his life to protect her eased Jesse's mind over her assumed past abuse.

Plus, Jesse told him if he ever did anything to make Pru unhappy, he'd kick him off the ship regardless of whether they were docked at a planet or not. Tarik's only response had been a cold calculating stare. Much like the one he currently gave Jesse.

"I was born on Segoha," Pru answered quietly. "I was once a member in good standing of the Saints of Aria. Eldest and only daughter of five in a prestigious family of very pious zealots steadfastly devoted to the planet's religion and belief system. I also ran away the night before I was to be married to a man older than my father. I can't go back. I *won't* go back."

Jesse was subdued listening to her confession. Pru hadn't said this much at one time about her past since she'd been his pilot. He smiled compassionately and responded, "Well, you don't have to go to the surface, Pru. You can stay here. I just need Tarik to—"

The shake of her head in the negative cut him off.

"The answer is no," Tarik reiterated, squeezing Pru's shoulder with a large calloused hand.

Jesse threw his hands in the air. "Why the hell not?"

"It's in your best interest, too," Pru exclaimed as unshed tears glistened in her green eyes.

Jesse took another deep calming breath before he turned to focus on Pru waiting on her explanation of why it was in his best interest not to go back. "Okay, clarify things for me."

"I stowed away on your ship. That's how I escaped Segoha. You were having a loud argument with the man chosen to be my husband.

He lectured you and your lengthy loud response distracted him so I could sneak on board your ship. I didn't want to marry Falke. He was cruel. Probably still is. You being on Segoha back then saved me. I hid for the entire two day trip.

"Later when the *Dragonfly* landed on Chronos, I was in the process of slipping off your ship when you found me and offered me food and later on a job as your pilot."

Jesse's nose wrinkled with distaste. He remembered Falke. What a bastard. "Geez, that ancient geezer was old enough to be your grandfather."

"The point is," Tarik reiterated, "we aren't going back there. It isn't safe for Pru. I won't allow it."

Jesse huffed sarcastically. "So are you forbidding this as my weapons officer or because of another more personal reason?"

Tarik pierced him with an intense stare for several seconds and finally shrugged. "Pick one. Either way, we aren't going."

"I'm the captain of this ship. I decide where we go and—"

"It isn't safe for you either, Jesse." Pru lifted her chin as if in defiance before he could finish his escalating lecture. She rose from her chair and took a step back to connect with Tarik's body. "My intended husband, Falke, knows that the *Dragonfly* was the only ship in the quadrant when I subsequently disappeared.

"I have no doubt the only thing that has kept him from hunting me down is their lack of the 'wicked' machinery necessary to chase a space cruiser. The Saints of Aria only allow very limited use of 'evil' technology."

Jesse stuck his finger over the tic which had just formed on his left eyelid. "Well then, you can stay on the ship, Pru. I'll deny ever knowing you existed. I don't care if they think I harbored you after my last visit, but I need to take Abigail back there. I promised her."

"I won't risk it." Tarik raised an eyebrow. Jesse recognized his unspoken signal of impending doom. Jesse wasn't too frightened.

"My new wife needs to go to Segoha. Therefore, I need to get there." Jesse turned to Tarik. "I was depending on you to back me up during the confrontation and negotiation with Abigail's former guardian."

Tarik shook his head glancing once at Pru with determination then back at Jesse. It was obvious his mind was made up. If Pru wasn't going, there was no way in two galaxies Tarik would go either.

Pru smiled at Tarik, but then her face sharpened into the definition of determination when she turned to face him. "I'm sorry, Jesse, anything else...anywhere else, and you know I'd follow you. But this, well...this is different. It's personal and I simply can't take a chance that Falke knows I'm alive."

Jesse took a different tack. It was time to calm everyone down. "A trip to Segoha is unexpected information. I know that. Let's sleep on it and we can discuss it further in the morning."

Tarik made a harrumph noise probably masking a growl, but he didn't respond. He and Pru left the room arm in arm.

Della and Tiger remained. Both were wide-eyed and surely waiting for the next installment of "what will this new wife do to tear apart the ship's crew."

Jesse needed Tarik to go with him to Segoha. He wanted someone he trusted to watch his back while negotiating the dowry payment listed in the proxy holder. The Saints of Aria didn't respect many things, but pure muscular might was one. He pulled Abigail's proxy document container out of his pocket and turned to his communications officer.

"Della, would you be opposed to looking over this document? I want to know beforehand what I can get away with." Jesse handed her the leather document container. "If we go to Segoha, I want to walk in holding all the cards, so to speak. Any financial ammunition you can find for me would be greatly appreciated."

"Sure, I'll take a look." Della smiled, pocketed the proxy and winked at him. She exited the room.

Tiger stood and stretched. "Well, that was an interesting meeting."

"Yeah. Whatever."

"See you in the morning, Captain."

Jesse nodded distractedly and left to go back to Abigail. He found he needed the comfort of a female. It occurred to him that if they didn't go to Segoha, Abigail would remain his responsibility, and his wife, permanently.

The heady idea of permanence with Abigail warred with his promise to release her and send her to another man.

Either way, he was likely screwed.

Chapter 10

Abigail was having a wonderful dream where a man she loved caressed her body and soul. Feelings of warmth, acceptance and love she'd never thought possible encompassed her spirit. She turned over expecting to find her dream lover, but she was instead troubled to find herself alone in a strange place. Naked.

She shot up brushing sleep from her eyes as she realized she was bare from head to toes beneath unfamiliar sheets. Grasping the thin soft coverings to her exposed breasts she tried to wake up. Saints above what had she done? Where was she?

Her gaze traveled around the room. Jesse's jacket came into view hanging on a hook across the room. Below it was her dress folded over a pile of discarded petticoats. Her dream lover truly existed outside her mind. He'd saved her. He'd taken her places she'd never dreamed existed. Wicked, wonderful places. Places she'd like to go to again.

Putting a hand up to one hot cheek she wondered if now that she'd crossed the boundary of propriety, could she ever be happy on the side of sheltered servitude? Likely not.

The door opened in a rush. Jesse filled the doorway a moment as a winsome smile lit his face when their eyes met. "You're awake."

Abigail clutched the sheets higher to hide her nudity. "Yes."

Jesse closed the door as he watched her. He didn't cross the room to join her on the bed as she expected, but leaned against the frame keeping a distance.

He inhaled a breath and his face turned serious as if he needed to say something distasteful. "I spoke to my crew about going to

Segoha."

She shifted the sheets against her throat and nodded. "How long until we get there?"

"The thing is…they won't go."

"I…what! Why not? You promised."

"I know I promised, but I can't fly the ship by myself. I need cooperation and some of the crew, come to find out, don't want to go to Segoha."

"I must get back there. My aunt—"

"I know." He cut her off with a shrug as if not too worried about his uncooperative crew. "We'll let them sleep on it and I'll bring it up again tomorrow morning. I'll take you to breakfast with me. Once they meet you, I'm sure we can work something out."

Jesse pulled a small package from his pocket and held it up for her inspection. "I brought you something to eat."

She frowned at the strange silver package the size of her palm. "What is it?"

"Nutrient bar."

Her brows crinkled in suspicion. He lifted himself slowly from the doorframe and approached her, holding out his offering.

"Thank you." Abigail took the square from his fingers making sure to keep her sheets in place. She stared at the square in puzzlement until he took it from her and opened the corner using his teeth. He offered her a bite. It tasted like sweetened oats glued together with honey syrup. She quickly finished the treat while he watched her clutching the sheets in place.

Seated on the edge of the bed, Jesse's arm went over her thighs. He rested a hand casually on the bed next to her hip. He leaned forward and his face came within inches of hers. "You don't have to protect yourself from me, Abigail. I've seen you. All of you."

Blood rushed to her face. She was loath to admit the feelings he drove in her. She wanted to reach out and touch him, but her confusion over the temporary nature of their relationship made her falter. The sheet clutching move was more to keep her hands from him than the other way around.

"You're beautiful. I want you every time I see you, but never fear that I'll take what you aren't willing to give."

She shook her head reluctant to ask for what she wanted. "As my husband, you have every right." *Please touch me.* "I was married before. I know what's expected of me." *Please, Jesse, touch me and I'll be yours whenever you want me for as long as you want me.*

He sighed. "How long before you figure out I'm not like your first husband?"

She cocked her head to the side. What was he up to? Surely he knew she had to obey even a temporary husband. How could she convince him to get intimate with her? "I've lived a very sheltered life—"

"I'm not buying it," he interrupted. "You stripped down to nothing and waited in my bed naked before you ever even knew me. You then offered yourself as payment for an accelerator module. I think you have a huge rebellious streak that you hide from most." He grinned engagingly. "But I'd kinda like to see it again."

He wanted her to show her rebellious streak? She wouldn't. If she let it have free rein, she'd never be able to stuff it down again. Once on Raylia, she'd have to hide it in the farthest reaches of her soul.

"As long as I'm your wife, I guess I could—"

"Bullshit. Do it because you want it not because of poor little pitiful you and your upbringing. Stand up for yourself for once, Abigail. Either you want me or you don't."

Abigail licked her lips attracting his stare. She had his undivided attention. She reconciled herself to the fact that eventually they'd go to Segoha and then she'd be headed for Raylia and a new husband. But until that time, she was Jesse's wife. His wife in all ways. And she wanted him. "I do want you…every time I see you."

Jesse grinned. "That wasn't hard to say, now was it?"

She smiled shyly. "Not too hard."

"Kiss me." He issued the command like a challenge. Would she boldly move forward and take his mouth in a seductive kiss? Her rebellious spirit burst free and she launched at him. She kissed him so hard their teeth clicked.

Jesse growled and kissed her back as the stab of his tongue between her lips sent a shower of sensation into her mouth. The sheet slipped and revealed her breasts. Soon Jesse had a handful of each one, which he palmed and stroked as he made love to her lips, thrusting and retreating until she wanted to scream in joy. She buried her fingertips in his soft hair twisting her mouth sideways to take in more.

Jesse broke the kiss. "Let's get in the shower."

"Shower? Now? Why?" *No. More touching, please.*

Jesse leaned in and teased her mouth with a chaste kiss. "The shower is a very sensual place, you know?" He kissed her lightly once again. The touch of his lips always made her skin tingle.

"It is?" Abigail hadn't tried a shower on Dooley's ship. Gravity showers were allowed by her sect, but at her parent's home she'd had a lovely soaking tub and servants to fill it.

Once she'd married the first time, a wooden tub bath had been all she could handle with her numerous and arduous chores. She'd hated bathing in the small tub, but at the end of her long day it was all she could manage before going to bed. She'd spent as long as she dared in the small wooden half drum filled with lukewarm water until the dreaded bedtime came. A bad memory she chose not to follow. Now she had Jesse. The awful part of her life with Myron was over.

Abigail sent her gaze to Jesse's expressive eyes. He was so handsome and gentle with her and everything she'd ever dreamed about in a future mate. She wished, and not for the first time, that he could be her permanent husband. She turned her complete attention to the here and now and quality time with Jesse.

"I'll wash you first. Then you can wash me." Jesse stroked a thumb across one sensitive nipple. His gaze never left her eyes.

The vision of what he suggested made her tingle from head to toes. After the shower it would be time for bed. She gazed into Jesse's eyes and realized for the first time that she didn't dread bedtime anymore.

She rose naked out of the bed and helped Jesse undress. He led her into the shower room. He had an automatic one with delicious water pressure. Forbidden on her planet.

Abigail stepped beneath the spray of the hot steamy water and an appreciative groan escaped her lips.

"That feels so good."

"I'll show you lots of things that feel good." Jesse moved into the shower space crowding her slightly. Anticipatory thrills of what he'd do to her ran down her spine, centering between her legs where a heavy ache of desire waited to be satisfied.

He grabbed her face with both hands and kissed her mouth softly. His hands slid from her neck to her shoulders and lower still. Knowing they were on a path to her sensitive breasts made her nipples harden. He stopped and reached for the soap then applied the slippery bar across her breasts soaping them up.

Jesse played on her chest lathering foam from neck to knees avoiding the space between her legs until she was forced to beg. "Please touch me, Jesse."

He put he soap back in the dish and whispered, "Where do you want me to touch you?"

Abigail bit her lip, closed her eyes and whispered, "Between my legs."

His hand traveled from her breast to the curls at the apex of her thighs. One finger slid between her legs and stroked the sensitive place there. Abigail shuddered so hard at his intimate touch, his hand slipped off the place she wanted him to rub.

"Do you want me to stroke you here?" His finger slid back to caress that blissful place again.

"Oh, yes." Back and forth, up and down, all around he rubbed until she knew the imminent explosion of pleasure was moments away. She put a hand up to the stall to balance herself and he stopped.

Her eyes popped open. "No. Don't stop."

He laughed. "Only for a moment. Would you be opposed to my cock coming inside you to play for awhile?"

"No." She felt the hot blush on her cheeks at the mention of the word "cock" even as she voiced her assent. She couldn't wait.

"Turn around. It will be better if I enter you from behind like when we were on my shuttle back on Delocia." Her memory slipped back to the lovely interlude on his shuttle, both in his bed and bent over the control panel of his ship.

Jesse shifted the stinging spray away from them. Abigail turned around, braced her arms on the walls of the shower and pushed her hips back into his body. His cock slid between her legs without entering her. He rubbed across her sensitive clit and she shuddered at the powerful sensation it drove. She glanced down between her legs to see the tip of his cock thrusting between her legs and with each swipe it tantalized her. Jesse's hand caressed her hip and suddenly slid into her view. His glorious hard cock entered her slick body all of a sudden and the fullness of him made her shudder in pleasure. Her body clenched around his cock trying to accommodate his size.

The hand on her hip slid forward between her legs and went directly to her clit. He stroked her only once. Watching him touch her sent an explosion of sensations radiating upward. She trembled. She shook. She screamed as the powerful release took her by surprise.

His other hand grabbed her other hip and he pumped inside of her again and again, thrusting deeply until one final thrust made a growl issue from his throat. He fell against her his chin resting on her shoulder, hugging her tight.

"You're the best wife," he murmured.

After he dried her off and carried her to bed, Jesse made love to her a second time. He kissed and touched her body for a long while as if worshipping it. The lights were low, but bright enough to watch him touch her everywhere.

When he finally mounted her, sliding his wonderful cock inside slowly, she moaned in a powerful rush of the climax enveloping her body. She hugged him close as he pumped sweetly and ever so leisurely inside of her quivering body, finally releasing on a deep sigh of pleasure.

Afterwards he left the lights on low and hugged her close in his sleep. Abigail stroked his soft hair wondering how she'd ever be able to allow another man to touch her.

She spent a restless night finally rising well before dawn to do the one thing which calmed her body and soul. She put on her dress and quietly slipped out of Jesse's room, but not before turning to watch him sleep for a couple of moments. He was the most magnificent man. She closed the door on a sigh and went to find the tools she needed to calm her riotous soul.

* * * *

The entire crew of the *Dragonfly* converged at the common room door at the same time Jesse arrived. He himself stumbled into the galley along with Tiger called by the siren fragrance wafting deliciously into every nook and cranny of every corridor on his ship.

Abigail was seated at the common room table surrounded by a bountiful array of food. *Home made food.* Jesse inhaled a deep appreciative lungful of the tantalizing aroma of home cooked goodies. "How did you get real supplies to cook with?"

Abigail jumped as if startled to see several hungry people around her. "I found them here in the kitchen area. I always cook to calm down. Plus, I thought I should contribute in some way…" She trailed off, staring at the horde of them.

"Well, let's eat then," Jesse announced.

Jesse and his crew sat down quickly looking over the selection of food as if trying to decide what to sample first. Tiger picked up what looked like a sweet bilberry muffin and murmured in awe, "We've never had anyone on board who could cook."

Abigail scrunched her brows. "What do you eat?"

"We get prepackaged food and heat it up."

Abigail wrinkled her nose. This accentuated her freckles and made Jesse want her, as usual.

Jesse leaned into Tiger and asked, "Where did we get all the cooking provisions?"

"We picked up some organic food supplies while you were on your secret run, Captain, but we hadn't traded it for prepackaged meals since we haven't gone anywhere yet." Tiger sniffed the muffin appreciatively. He took a bite and Jesse thought Tiger's eyes were going to roll back in his head. Soon he moaned in pleasure as he chewed.

Tiger popped his eyes back open. "This is the best food I've ever eaten," he told Abigail with a lovesick smile on his face.

Soon plates and bowls were passed around the table and one by one his crew started moaning in delight. Jesse speared a sausage patty. Taking a bite, the seasoned flavors melted in his mouth and he too joined them in moaning appreciation.

Abigail had a surprised look on her face. "I'm so glad you all like it," she said quietly as they consumed every morsel she'd prepared. "My first husband never cared for my cooking abilities."

"This first husband of yours," Pru wiped her mouth after a sip of coffee, "was he old enough to be your grandfather?"

Abigail sat a moment as if stunned, then responded, "No. He was old enough to be my grandfather's older brother."

Pru laughed out loud. She sobered quickly and asked, "So why do you want to go back there so bad."

"My Aunt Eugenia is still there. I want to ensure she wasn't put into an elder house." Pru blanched at the mention of elder house. Jesse remained silent as he ate and watched his crew. He genuinely hoped that Abigail might persuade them to take a trip to Segoha and fulfill his promise.

"My guardian Pitney has no compassion. He expects me to be on Raylia by now only I don't have valid proxy papers. I'm certain my aunt is already at the elder house." Abigail glanced at Jesse once and lowered her head. "But Jesse saved me by doing it. Otherwise I'd be in jail for a murder I didn't commit. But I still want to get her out of there if I can."

Pru sighed. "I visited my grandma in an elder house once. A rabid animal deserves a better home than that evil place." She took a deep breath and announced, "So, we can't have your Aunt stay one minute longer than necessary in one."

Jesse blinked. "What are you saying?"

Pru drilled him a determined glare. "It means I'll set a course for Segoha. Then I'll set up an oxygen tank in your hidden compartments to hide in once we are within sensory range. Jesse, you'll have to pilot the ship into the dock."

"Pru, we don't have to go." Tarik put an arm across her shoulders.

Pru turned, leaned into him and smiled. "We do. But it's okay. Please go with him, Tarik. Just make sure that if my name comes up, you tell them I was discovered dead stowed away on your ship. They don't have the technology to check further than how many people are on board, but they will likely ask you about me. They hate it when anyone escapes. Especially women."

Jesse understood her state of mind when he'd first met her. She had been abused by the very family supposed to protect her. "I promise we won't let them find you. I'll fly us in and communicate with them so they won't even have your voice on record, okay?"

Pru and Tarik exchanged glances again. She nodded and slid her arms around Tarik's waist. They held each other for a long while.

Jesse relaxed for the first time since bringing Abigail aboard.

Chapter 11

Abigail cleaned up the breakfast dishes with Tiger's help. The rest of the crew discussed strategy in the common room and plotted the details of what would happen once they arrived at Segoha.

"Once we're cleared to land," Jesse explained, "Abigail and I will go directly to her guardian's house to get the new documents. I'll volunteer to take her to Raylia.

"Meanwhile, Della and Tiger will say they are leaving the ship to gather supplies, when in fact they will stand by if needed and retrieve Abigail's aunt if I can't find a way to have her released to my care. Hopefully, we can all meet back at the *Dragonfly* without shooting our way out in a gun battle."

Della started to speak next, but noticed Abigail and smiled instead remaining quiet.

Abigail stood in the doorway a moment. "I'd like to thank you all for doing this. I truly appreciate it." A few nodded and others merely smiled.

"I'll leave you all to make plans." She caught Jesse's gaze and motioned that she was returning to his room. He smiled in return, waved at her once and continued plotting with his crew. Abigail was so grateful for their help. Even if her aunt was in an elder house, she wouldn't be there for much longer.

"I looked over the proxy document, Jesse. I may have something for you to negotiate with," Della said as Abigail left the room.

* * * *

Three days into the trip to Segoha, Jesse arrived at his room with an idea to share with Abigail. He didn't know if she'd be interested, but held high hopes that her rebellious streak came with added curiosity.

He entered the room with anticipation coloring his attitude. "Abigail?"

"In here," she called from the direction of the bathroom. Jesse heard a splash and found Abigail reclining neck deep in his bubble-filled bathtub.

"Still like the tub better than the shower, huh?"

She grinned. "I had a bathtub like this when I lived with my parents." Her sudsy arms came out of the water briefly to tease him before submerging again. "This one is much easier to fill and use."

Jesse strolled closer and sat on the edge of the tub hoping to see more flesh. The lure of her innocence sometimes startled his reason. He'd never been married until Lola, a sham union probably shouldn't count. Time spent with Abigail, after a long shift running the ship, was fast becoming his favorite part of the day. The knowledge of her being his wife warmed his soul.

He lowered one hand into the warm water and scooped up a handful of bubbles. "Are you going to invite me in there with you?"

A sharp intake of breath accompanied the scarlet color tinting her cheeks. Even after the half week they'd spent together living as husband and wife, she was still shy. Well, she was always shy at first, but then warmed up once they got into bed.

"Do you…" She paused and inhaled deeply as if the extra air would strengthen her resolve to finish answering. "Do you want to come in to the tub?"

"Oh, yes."

A grin slid into place. "Please join me then."

Jesse unfolded his arms and stood. He shed his clothes slowly as she watched out of the corner of her eye. The color of her face deepened as each article of clothing hit the floor.

Once naked, Jesse stepped into the fragrant bubbled bath and stood above his gorgeous wife. Their time together had been limited, and if all went according to plan, they'd likely end up separated very soon. He contemplated what it would be like to come to his quarters alone. No Abigail to greet him anymore. Sadness invaded his thoughts but Jesse quickly tamped them down in favor of making plans for the immediate future.

"Let me slip in behind you, darlin'."

Abigail shifted forward to allow him access. Sliding beneath the water, Jesse couldn't control his randy cock which had grown thicker with each moment spent in her company. Wedged against soft female flesh, it was a wonder he didn't permanently dent her spine.

Jesse settled down into the tub and got comfortable. "So tell me about your past experience."

"What experience?"

"Sexual experience."

She stiffened against him, but he pulled her slick shoulders and settled her head beneath one side of his collarbone. "I was married for a very short time to an old man. It was unsatisfying. What else do you want to know?"

"I'd like to know a little more about the rebellious streak you have and where it came from. You must have seen or done something to understand what happens between a man and a woman before you were married to know it was unsatisfying."

"Perhaps."

"Tell me about it."

"I can't."

"Sure you can. This conversation is just between you and me. And I won't tell. A man and his wife can share anything regardless of how long their union lasts."

A sigh escaped but she started talking is a low tone. "I saw the stable hand and the cook together when I was sixteen years old."

"Oh? What were they doing?"

Each question he asked brought a deeper blush to her lovely freckled skin than the one before. Again, her near whispered response floated to his waiting ears. "I was in the stable visiting my horse, but I was supposed to be resting up for a party my guardian was hosting later in the evening. I didn't want to go to the party so I rebelled and snuck out my bedroom window and went to the barn. Before Dustin and Mary came into the barn, I contemplated the punishment I'd receive for galloping away on my horse and the merits of doing it anyway."

"Why? Parties can be fun." Jesse stroked a fingertip along her soft shoulder on a path to the sensitive spot below her ear.

"Not this one. It was a selection party. A group of eligible unattached men from the Saints of Aria would come over and stare at me to see if I interested any of them as a future wife. Every one was old and decrepit. I wasn't interested in having them leer at me for an entire evening."

Jesse's eyes mashed shut in anger at the practices of a strict religion he didn't want to understand. "What happened in the stable?"

Abigail cleared her throat and continued. "I was about to saddle my horse, but the back door to the stable popped open and scared me. I ducked down in the stall to hide.

"Through the slats I could see Dustin and Mary enter through the door. They were hugging, kissing and putting their hands all over each other as they stumbled across the room toward a bale of still bundled hay. I couldn't leave without them seeing me so I stayed hidden."

"And did you have a clear view of what they were doing?"

"Yes," she whispered. Her tone had softened and yet he felt her body stiffen slightly against him. "As they kissed, they pulled at each others clothing until most was stripped away."

Jesse trailed his fingers along her shoulder and down one arm in an effort to calm her. "What happened next?"

"Dustin still had pants on, but he put his shirt on the bail of hay and kissed Mary. She lay back on Dustin's shirt and pulled her skirt up. Not only wasn't she wearing a shirt any more, but she also wasn't wearing any under things.

"He pulled his pants down to his mid thighs. I could see part of his bottom."

"Could you see his cock?"

Another whispered, "yes," came out softly.

"He stuck it into Mary and she moaned. Dustin put his hands on her bare breasts and pinched her nipples which made her moan louder. She didn't seem to be in pain and then he thrust his hips forward over and over again. Mary called his name again and again. She reached down and put her hands on his hips to pull him inside her body even harder."

Jesse cupped one of Abigail's breasts and ran his thumb across her nipple. Her back arched and a thin hiss of pleasure escaped her lips.

"And then?" He tugged at the one nipple as she drew in a long shaky breath.

"Mary's back suddenly arched and she groaned loudly. Dustin grabbed her thighs in each of his hands and kept thrusting and thrusting inside her until he stiffened and growled. They both panted like they'd been running. He bent at the waist and covered Mary. She held him tight and stroked his hair. She told him that she loved him and he lifted up to stare into her eyes when he told her that he loved her, too."

"Did watching them turn you on?"

Abigail stilled. "I don't know what you mean." The skin on her shoulders flushed to scarlet, and he knew she understood.

"Yes, you do." Jesse slipped his other hand to cover both breasts. Her pert nipples dented his palms. "Did you feel a rush in your body? Did your womb tighten? Did you get wet?" He sent one hand careening across her belly to dive between her legs as he kissed the back of her neck.

His fingers dancing over her clit as she murmured, "What are you doing to me?"

"Pleasurable things." Jesse tugged at one nipple and stroked her clit beneath the warm water. The bubbles had faded until he could see most of her lovely body. After only three or four moments of massaging her clit, she stiffened and a short scream erupted. He lifted her body and realigned his hips so that his cock rested at the entrance of her pussy. But he didn't enter her. She hadn't ever denied him, but he was careful to ensure his advances were welcomed each and every time they came together.

Abigail's head fell back against his shoulder. "Do it. Come inside of me. I need you."

Jesse thrust his hips up pushing inside her warm pulsing pussy. The remnants of her climax gripped his dick in rhythmic pleasure. Waves of bubbly water sloshed around them and over the edge of the tub onto the floor with each movement of his cock entering her body. Stroke. Splash. Stroke. Splash.

Humid air swirled between them. Jesse breathed in the clean, damp scent of her hair and pushed his cock deeper still. A powerful orgasm released with his next breath. He clutched Abigail's shoulders to his chest as the rush of pleasure tingled from his hips all the way through to the tip of his cock.

"You do the most amazing things to me." Abigail sagged against him. He slid his arms around her and settled her against his chest.

"I aim to please." With a soft kiss to her neck, Jesse sank into the warmth of the water nearly devoid of bubbles, holding her close and wondering how he'd ever live without her. Shoulders resting along the edge of the tub, Jesse released a deep breath, ruffling her hair.

"I shouldn't feel the way I do." Abigail twisted her head to one side and pressed an ear against his chest.

"Why not? We aren't doing anything wrong."

A soft sigh escaped her lips and brushed her breath across his flat nipple. "*You* aren't."

"Neither are you."

"In your world."

"In many worlds."

"I don't know any other worlds. I've only lived on Segoha. Well, except for the short time on Dooley's ship." Her fingers traced an invisible line from his shoulder to the inside of his elbow and back up again. "That was quite an education in and of itself."

"I'll bet. Did he have a VR cube?"

"I don't know. What is it?"

"Virtual reality room." He stroked her soft, sun-kissed locks from the crown of her head past her shoulders and down to her belly button.

Eyebrows arched, Abigail rolled her head onto his shoulder seeking his eyes before answering quietly. "I don't even know what that is or if Dooley had one. If he did, I never saw it."

"It's a room where you can visualize and experience other worlds, other sights, and other pleasures. It's a power hog on most space craft and usually regulated, but well worth it in my opinion." Jesse grinned. "Lucky for you I've got a VR room on my ship. And luckier still, I've got some time earned in there. I'll show you firsthand what it is."

"Right now?"

"Why not?"

She shrugged and smiled. The trust shining in her face touched him. Part of his intent was to open her eyes to the varied worlds in this solar system she'd never dreamed of viewing. The other intent was purely sexual.

The *Dragonfly* currently sped on a course to her hostile home planet where antiquated ideas passed for a lifestyle only conducive to half the population. Perhaps he could convince her there were other options besides the one she was driven to complete. Perhaps he could show her a different way of life. Perhaps he should keep his ideas to himself and not give her more than she bargained for in this transaction.

Abigail stood with her arms covering her breasts. Streams of water and leftover bubbles slid down her lovely body into the tub. Jesse enjoyed the view for a slow count of ten before rising to help her dry off. He wanted to make love to her again, but decided to wait and enjoy her in the VR room. Anticipation filled him with lustful thoughts of their immediate future.

Fantasy mixed with technology made for a powerful aphrodisiac.

Chapter 12

Ten minutes later, Jesse led her down a quiet hallway. He'd put her in his oversized robe, but she only wore sheer underpants beneath it. She wasn't sure where they were going and truthfully, she wasn't sure if she wanted to experiment. He wouldn't explain or say anything further about the "place" beyond, "You have to see it to understand."

After a short walk, Jesse stopped before a large metal door. He put his palm on the flat screen by the door's small square window. The space beneath his hand lit up with an orange glow, and after a soft beeping noise, the door latch released, shifting open a few inches. They entered a small dimly lit room. There was a closed door directly across from the entry. She took another step inside. To the left was a narrow bench and across on the opposite wall were shoulder height double clothing hooks.

Abigail wrapped her arms around her waist at the prospect of losing her clothing.

"How does this work?" Her apprehension was palpable.

"Don't be frightened. Tell you what. We'll start with something non-threatening. This device was originally invented to bring history to those unable to remember. Are there any far off worlds you've always wanted to see? Old or new, doesn't matter." He stood before a control panel with a plethora of lights and buttons.

She shrugged. "Ancient Earth is the only one I'm familiar with besides the planets in this system. From what little I've heard I don't want to see any of the neighboring worlds as they're all visually the same desolate plains as Segoha and Delocia."

"That is likely true. Besides, Earth is a very popular VR program.

I'll set it for the quick world tour and reserve the rest of the time for us."

Abigail nodded, but didn't truly understand. She trusted Jesse and allowed herself to relax a little. "All right."

Jesse removed her robe, but left her most intimate undergarment in place. He proceeded to put a series of adhesive patches on various places over her body. One went on her neck, another over her heart and one on either side of her temples. He helped her shrug the robe back on and led her to another room. The space was dark with very tiny pinpricks of light spaced evenly. Once they stepped inside it was difficult to judge how big the room was.

Abigail slipped closer to Jesse and slid her hands to his waist. Her fingertips brushed the elastic of the loose pants he wore.

"Close your eyes for a moment," he whispered. "Don't be afraid," he added when she tensed and sucked up to his side.

Abigail closed her eyes and after a few seconds she heard the unusual sound of water falling. Her eyes popped open to a breathtaking view of a waterfall. Positioned at the base of the wondrous sight, moist air circulated around them as if they had been transported to another planet.

"It's so beautiful. What is this place?"

"This waterfall is called Yosemite Falls. It's from ancient earth in a place called California."

The sheer face of the rock above was split in two by the narrow fast pulsing stream of white frothing water flowing from the gap between two rock faces. The flow of water fell an impossibly long way before crashing at the rocky surface below. Abigail thought it was the most magnificent scene she'd ever witnessed.

After only a couple of minutes the scenery around them melted into something totally different. Suddenly they stood in a clearing surrounded by lush green plants and forests all around and above. The floral scent of thousands of flowers perfumed the air all around them made a sigh emit after she inhaled the lovely fragrance. Everywhere she looked there was a blast of color and more green than she'd ever seen in one place in all her life.

Abigail heard whistling and the noise of calls from strange unseen animals. She moved closer to Jesse. "This is called a rain forest. It smells earthy and floral. The sounds you hear are from the birds and wildlife from that time."

"They won't pop out and scare us or chase after us, will they?"

He squeezed her arm reassuringly. "No. I have this program set to sensory only. I'll be interactive, but I won't set it to 'surprise mode' this time."

"Surprise mode?"

"Well, sometimes it's exciting if you know what is coming, but not when to expect it."

"I'm not really in the mood for surprises, is that okay?"

"Absolutely. We can save that for another time." He grinned.

She relaxed and turned in a circle to see the full view. "It's lovely. Thank you." Abigail leaned her head on his shoulder. He slid an arm around her back and held her close.

"What's next?"

"Glacier Lakes."

The scene around them dissolved once again and they stood before a large lake. In the distance, white capped mountains hovered along the horizon like a mystical dream. The water was so smooth an upside down image of the mountains reflected in the lake. The temperature around them was decidedly cold.

Segoha never reached a temperature below seventy degrees. Being in an environment chilly enough to see the breath coming from your lips was a new life experience she tucked away with a delighted sigh.

Five scenes later they returned for a final look at the waterfall only this time they were closer to the water. They were so close to the pool where the end of the water fell, Abigail wondered if she'd be able to reach out and touch the spray of water. Jesse reached out first and splashed her. She squealed in delight and reached out to splash him in return.

"This is amazing. I love the VR cube."

"Just wait. It gets even better."

Around her the scene changed again and she sucked in a shocked breath as the barn from her childhood took shape around her down to her horse, Lucky, neighing softly in the stall behind her. "This is exactly the stables from my home on Segoha. How did you reconstruct it so perfectly?"

"The adhesive patches I stuck to your temples can read images and memories with a fair degree of accuracy."

"I'll say." She inhaled a deep breath. "It even smells the same."

Jesse took her in his arms and kissed her mouth tenderly. "I want you to enjoy this. Please allow yourself the pleasure."

"What do you mean?"

"Remember we are in a virtual reality cube. Everything will seem very real. The sights. The smells. The touching. But it's just a fantasy, right? Anything goes here. But if something makes you unhappy, just say stop program." Jesse peeled off the robe she wore and only her panties remained. Those were slid off next and deposited behind her. The exhilarating idea of being naked while she watched a seductive memory from her past sent her blood racing through her veins.

"Okay. I'm ready."

Jesse said aloud, "Run program J dash A One."

Abigail stood in the stall of the barn from her childhood home as if eight years had melted away and disappeared. Jesse slid behind her and put his hands at her waist and his chin on her shoulder.

Seconds later, a familiar sound registered. Someone was coming. Abigail reflexively tried to squat down, but Jesse stopped her. "No one can see us. Relax. Watch. Enjoy."

The wooden barn door opened slowly. Dustin, the stable hand from her uncle's household, entered the rustic barn and ushered Mary, the cook's assistant, inside. He looked out the slit in the door one last time at presumably her uncle's house and turned to Mary with a big grin.

"Just the two of us," Dustin said with a smile. Mary giggled and tilted her head back to look in Dustin's eyes.

Abigail pressed her shoulders against Jesse's chest still unconvinced that this voyeuristic view was hidden from the other participants. His hands came around her waist in a reassuring squeeze. She shifted her gaze back to the couple about to embark on the first sexual act Abigail had ever witnessed.

Mary threw her skinny arms around Dustin's neck and kissed him with a passion Abigail remembered with heart-pounding clarity. His roughened hands clutched Mary's tiny waist and after a few moments he lifted her off of her feet to place her near the bale of hay. As in her memory, Dustin removed his shirt, exposing his muscular tanned back and spread it across the top of the hay bale for Mary. The peasant blouse was pushed off of her shoulders exposing her small pert breasts. Dustin made a noise of approval as he latched his mouth to the tip of one of Mary's breasts.

Abigail's nipples tightened as if she were the one being sucked on. With a clearer view of the long ago young lovers, Abigail watched with rapt attention as the scene progressed exactly as she remembered down to the finest detail. The arousing sounds they made as they came together, the sheen of sweat on Dustin's back as he thrust into Mary, and the scent of leather and hay all around her made for a sharp recollection. Watching this memory made Abigail desire the same action with Jesse.

As if he read her mind, Jesse slid his hands up her torso to cup her sensitive breasts. She swayed against him with a sudden and sharp fission of arousal stretching from her aching nipples to her core.

Jesse's chin pushed into her shoulder and as he gently stroked her peaks. "Is it like you remembered?"

"Yes. Exactly."

"Spread your legs apart. Let me touch you."

She widened her stance and allowed Jesse's fingers access to her most private place. Another thrill rippled across her body as he touched her clit. She inhaled sharply as pleasure radiated outward from between her legs.

The carnal sex scene in the barn continued until Mary cried out in pleasure and Dustin pumped one final time into her body before collapsing against her, bent over Mary and still intimately connected.

"That was sexy."

"Yes." Abigail tried to turn around in his arms, but Jesse held her in place.

"Wait. Keep watching them. I have an idea."

"What?"

"In your memories did you ever want Dustin to do that to you?"

"I…no…well…maybe."

"Would you like for Dustin to join us?"

"I…yes." Abigail's heart pounded so furiously at the idea of what he suggested, it was a wonder it didn't burst from her chest.

"Initiate interface for program J dash A One," Jesse called out.

Before them, the scene melted to show only Dustin. Mary was gone and so was the side of the stall which had protected her from view so long ago. Shirt still off, Dustin turned and fastened his pants. He grinned and approached Abigail with a wolfish expression.

"What will he do?"

"He's going to join us."

Abigail went rigid at the thought and Jesse kissed the back of her neck. "Relax."

She took a deep breath and released it. "I'll try."

Dustin strolled over and cupped Abigail's face in his hands. He leaned in and kissed her lips once gently before he trailed light kisses across her face, down her neck and headed for her breasts. He tasted like coffee and something sweet. Her body pulsed with arousal.

Jesse's hands moved away from her nipples, so Dustin could take first one tip and then the other into his warm mouth. Abigail's back arched as if to allow deeper suction from Dustin's mouth. It was amazing and even with her eyes closed, it felt completely real.

Abigail shivered with desire. Jesse's hands rested on her hips. She felt his hard cock digging into her backside. The sudden urge to feel him deeply inside her compelled her to speak.

"Jesse." She reached a hand around to caress his shaft through the single layer of fabric he wore. "I want you inside of me."

"Happy to oblige you, darlin'." His whispered voice added a layer of sensual arousal. He slid his pants down only enough to free his shaft as Dustin alternated sucking on her nipples to her delight.

Jesse brushed the head of his cock along her butt cheek before sliding it between her legs. The hard hot shaft graced the opening of her body and a gush of moisture from her nether folds greeted his overture. He grasped her hips and began a slow massage putting the tip of his cock across her wet slit.

"Inside," she turned her head and whispered. The impatient tone of her voice came through in husky fashion.

A low laugh issued from Jesse's throat. He shifted his stance and entered her body with a short thrust. One man had his cock inside her pussy as another man sucked on her nipples. Abigail's senses were on overload.

"Lick her clit while I fuck her," Jesse said to Dustin over her shoulder. Dustin didn't hesitate, but shifted his lips to kiss her lower and lower. Jesse's fingertips took over the job of stimulating her nipples as Dustin kissed her belly and then put his mouth over the mound at the apex of her legs.

Jesse's cock thrust inside her pussy as Dustin licked her clitoris once. The pure pulse of pleasure which issued forth almost brought Abigail to he knees. She swayed in Jesse's arms, but he held her up.

Dustin brushed his hot tongue over her clit again and Jesse groaned in her ear. "Can you feel his tongue on your clit?"

"Yes." Her response a low hiss of pleasure.

"Do you like it?"

"Yes. Oh!" Dustin grasped her hips and his tongue and lips began a fevered assault of her clit. He sucked and licked. The idea of Jesse's cock being so close made her wonder if he could feel Dustin's tongue as he moved inside her.

Her mouth voiced the question aloud before prudence could stop it. "Can you feel his tongue on your shaft?"

Jesse pinched both of her nipples, thrust deeply into her pussy and whispered, "Yes. I feel him licking both you and me every time I thrust inside your hot pussy. It's indescribably pleasurable."

Dustin wiggled his tongue against her clit with delicious pressure as Jesse pushed his cock harder and faster inside her pussy. The sensations convulsed across her pelvis and breasts until a familiar feeling enveloped her in rapturous warmth.

Abigail opened her mouth and screamed as her climax registered hard and heavy in her womb. She shrieked again as Jesse thrust impossibly deep one more time at the moment she slipped into oblivion. He stiffened behind her and buried his face into her neck. Dustin kissed his way back up her body and moved one of Jesse's hands from her breast. He licked the tip of her nipple and she shuddered with the most acute pleasure she'd ever imagined.

Jesse's arms circled her waist as his hot breath ruffled the hair near one ear.

"Amazing," he panted. "Fucking amazing."

She giggled. Dustin released his mouth from her breast and stood to his full height. He leaned in and kissed her mouth. She could taste the musky flavor of her own body on his lips and another delightful shudder rocked her body from the memory of where his mouth had just been. It was difficult for her to believe this wasn't really happening.

"Say goodbye to Dustin," Jesse whispered as his panting slowed.

Dustin grinned and blew a kiss.

"Goodbye, Dustin." Abigail smiled as he faded away, leaving only the two of them.

"I want to put you on that bale of hay and recreate what we

watched earlier."

Abigail looked over to where Dustin's shirt still rested on the bale. "Okay."

They strolled naked over to the hip high surface.

"Turn around and lay down."

Abigail turned but kissed him first before settling back on the bale. She'd barely put her shoulders horizontal when Jesse grasped her hips and slid his hard cock deeply into her pussy with one deep thrust.

His hands rested on hips so she grabbed his forearms for something to hang onto as he pushed in and out of her body. One of his hands shifted to the space between her legs. He rubbed her clit with his thumb as he thrust deeper and deeper inside her pussy. She gazed up at the man she'd fallen in love with as the tickle of pre-orgasm fluttered across her skin. In the next moment a pounding climax rolled across her body. Her back arched and she called Jesse's name out loud. She inhaled the combined scent of fresh hay and the musky scent of their lovemaking into a new memory she knew she'd never in her lifetime ever forget.

She pushed out a long breath and searched Jesse's face to memorize every wonderful vision of this moment.

Jesse caught her gaze with his own and whispered, "I love you, Abigail." His eyes then dipped half closed and he stiffened after one last deep thrust of his cock. The pleasurable growl signaling his climax washed through her with stunning clarity as his words blazed a trail across her conscious.

He loved her. And she loved him, too.

Abigail hugged him tight when he leaned over and pushed his chest into hers.

She longed to respond to his declaration, but the nearing prospect of her desolate future life pummeled her brain. She couldn't love him or she'd never be able to leave him to go to Raylia.

Saying the words out loud might deter her from her ultimate goal.

She couldn't let her aunt languish in an elder home to satisfy her dream of love.

* * * *

Jesse took a deep breath and clicked the ship to shore radio. "Segoha Prime, this is *Dragonfly* transport requesting permission to land."

Several moments later a scratchy crackling response came. "*Dragonfly* transport, what business do you have with our citizens?"

"We'd like to discuss transport business potential and additionally, we have one of your citizens aboard needing a visit with her family."

This time the pause lasted longer. Jesse opened his mouth and prepared to demand an answer, when a response came. "What citizen of Segoha do you harbor on your vessel?"

"Formerly Miss Abigail Deveronne now Mrs. Pelland, since she got married." Jesse wasn't bringing up Pru's name and hoped they didn't impound his craft in an effort to look for her.

The silence continued for much too long. Jesse didn't know whether it was due to the *Dragonfly* and suspected stealer of one Prudence Brock his pilot or because of the fact that Abigail was supposed to be married to someone on Raylia by now. Instead she was married to him, an outworlder of the most wicked variety.

The Saints of Aria would likely determine that he was the kind of man who seduced prim and proper girls from Segoha to experience immoral sinful things. And Abigail had been seduced, repeatedly and with great vocal relish on this much too short journey to her home. The time they'd spent in the VR room was hands down the most erotic he could have ever imagined.

Jesse and Abigail spent the past two weeks of the journey in each others arms whenever possible. The sex was phenomenal. Jesse was loath to admit he would miss Abigail once the deal on Segoha wrapped up. Without telling Abigail, he set the program to also record their time together in the VR room. He wanted the memory available if something happened and they ended up apart.

The strategy he had in store for the folks on Segoha, especially Abigail's former guardian, Pitney, were not carved in stone.

Anything unexpected might happen and along with his somewhat reluctant crew, Jesse was prepared for a couple eventualities. But on the remote chance of success, he pressed forward with his secret course of action.

The crackling voice came back. "*Dragonfly* transport, you may dock in bay five. Prepare to be boarded by Segoha Defense."

"Roger that, heading to bay five."

"You'd better hope they don't find Pru," Tarik warned in a tight low voice. He bent and loomed over Jesse seated in the pilot's chair. "She also better have enough oxygen or I'll kill you with my bare hands."

"Noted. She'll be fine. One crisis at a time, Tarik. I need to focus."

Tarik merely grunted in response.

The Segoha Defense officers who boarded did a weak cursory check through the entire ship. They had no penetrating radar equipment and Pru wasn't found. But after a nod from the leader of the group Abigail was surrounded and one of them put manacles on her wrists.

Jesse approached the loose circle crowding her. "Hey, what do you think you're doing? Get away from my wife."

The leader of the group of officers pulled out a document and began reading. "Miss Abigail Deveronne, formerly known as Abigail Smedly, you've been charged with a crime and are sought in reference to the death of your husband, Myron Smedly."

The security officer, who had locked her in irons before Jesse could move to stop it, ignored Jesse's outburst and further stated, "You'll be sequestered in Segoha jail until such time proof of your innocence in this very serious matter of your husband's death can be established."

"Wait a minute. I'm her husband."

The leader's upper lip curled. "How is that possible, sir?"

Jesse whipped out the proxy document and opened it for him to read.

The lead officer gave him a tight lipped smile. "Well, this is highly irregular. We'll have to contact Miss Deveronne's former guardian, Mr. Pitney, and have him explain this document. In the meantime, you'll still be required to go to the jail until the charges are straightened out."

Tarik moved forward. "Then you can take me with you. I'm her bodyguard. I'll see to it that nothing happens to my captain's valuable property."

The lead security officer took a step backward. "Thank you, but that won't be necessary."

"I wasn't asking permission." Tarik took another step forward until he crowded the officer holding Abigail's bindings.

Jesse nodded once at the lead officer. "Remove the irons. She won't need them." He paused a moment and added, "That also wasn't a request."

The leader sighed deeply and nodded at one of his men and the irons came off her wrists.

The leader added, "As her husband, you may go with her, but sequestering a female alone with another male who is not a family member is forbidden."

Tarik growled at the lead defense officer and Jesse thought the man might wet himself.

"Guess we're all going together then." Jesse squeezed between two of the men surrounding Abigail and grabbed her hand. He brought it to his lips and kissed the back of her fingertips. "Because I won't abandon my wife to the likes of you."

The senior officer engaged in a staring contest for a moment before nodding his head at his men. A public display of affection was a big no-no here, but he dared them to cross Tarik. They relaxed their guard around Abigail. En masse they exited the *Dragonfly* to Dock Five and headed directly to the Segoha security authority.

Once inside the primitive one story building, the three of them were led to a holding room with a wooden table and several chairs and not a jail cell.

"If you hadn't come with me, I'd be behind bars." Abigail seated herself on a hard wooden chair. Jesse plopped down beside her and grabbed her hand.

Tarik exhaled a long sigh and leaned against a wooden wall. "I'm not thrilled to be here."

"I'm shocked," Jesse said sarcastically. "I thought you were using your happy growl today."

Tarik grunted. "Do we even know what we're waiting for?"

"Probably a Segoha Committee member." Abigail squeezed his hand. "Or my guardian. Or both. Depends on who leveled the charge of murder against me for Myron."

They didn't have long to wait.

Abigail put a death lock on his fingers as a tall foreboding figure dressed in black entered the room.

"Abigail." The man drilled her with an angry stare. "You have a lot of explaining to do."

She tried to stand, but Jesse stopped her. She was also about to answer, but Jesse squeezed her hand once before releasing it.

He stood fixing a glare on Pitney. "She only explains things to me."

The stranger's dark gaze settled on him and his expression said he found Jesse lacking. "And you are?"

"I'm her husband."

Pitney's face hardened into an unreadable mask. "Impossible."

"No. Improbable perhaps, but definitely a reality."

The man shifted his gaze to Abigail. He sneered and said,

"Abigail, tell your 'husband' who I am."

"I don't care who you are unless you're providing Abigail's dowry. That's why I'm here. To collect."

Pitney's face morphed into one of understanding. "Why you insufferable greedy blackmailer."

"Sticks and stones. Are you Pitney?"

The man stiffened. "I am."

"Good. Then you owe me several thousand credits." Jesse pulled the proxy document protector and waved it.

Pitney's eyes gave him away. Jesse knew he recognized it, but said in a seething tone. "I most assuredly do not owe you anything."

"I have a proxy document sighed by you, and now me," Jesse pointed to his chest, "which states Abigail's husband of more than seven days, again that's me," Jesse pointed to his chest yet again, "will share in the trust fund left to one Abigail Deveronne, now Abigail Pelland, by her late parents." He pointed at Abigail once and turned back to face an angry Pitney.

Abigail reacted as expected. She sat straight up and asked, "My parents left me money?"

"Shut up, Abigail!" Pitney shouted.

"Do not talk to my wife like that again," Jesse spoke in his most lethal tone, "or I'll have my bodyguard tear off one of your arms."

Tarik growled. It definitely wasn't his happy growl. Pitney took a step backwards.

"How could you possibly know about the trust fund?" Pitney shot an angry glance to Abigail.

Jesse smiled in triumph. "She doesn't know. My communications officer went over the proxy document carefully. She found several interesting things once we hacked into your records. Lots of irregularities I'm sure the Saints of Aria would find all of it very fascinating. The most astonishing is the secret connection you have to Raylia."

Pitney blanched. "How could you possibly breech my records?"

"People not well versed in electronic information tend to miss key facts when conducting business. Especially illegal business," Jesse explained condescendingly.

"You married Abigail off to Myron because he relinquished any hold on her extensive funds. He gave you power over her trust fund for a nominal fee. Once they'd been married for seven days the deal would have been set. Myron would have a gorgeous wife far too young for him and you would have her money. But things didn't work out for you as planned, did they, Pitney?

"When Myron died before the stated and agreed upon one week of marriage, it threw a wrench into your plans. You quickly arranged another marriage to someone on the other side of the solar system so you'd again have control over all those lovely credits."

"You're mad." Pitney sneered. "You have no proof."

"Oh, but I do. You had Abigail shipped off to far away Raylia so when the barristers came to inform her of her wealth, she'd no longer be on the planet to stop you from taking charge of her estate. I'm sure you have a barrister or two in your pocket, as well."

Abigail was obviously in shock. Her mouth hung open. "What are you talking about?"

"Your guardian shipped you across the galaxy so you wouldn't have a voice in your own accounts."

She shook her head. "But how could I have a voice?"

"Your parents wrote their will with very specific stipulations. You were supposed to be allowed to marry for love. Their last will and testament gave you the financial clout within the Saints of Aria to do so, but apparently they died before telling anyone. I'm sorry Abigail but all the money he has is really yours."

Abigail stood and faced Pitney red faced with anger. "How could you?"

Pitney was apparently not moved by her anger. "Easily. I assure you."

"I went willingly to Raylia so I could go before the Common

Guild as per your demand in order to save Aunt Eugenia," Abigail snarled. "But I could have stayed and taken care of her myself with *my* own credits if you weren't so evil."

Jesse started coughing.

Pitney shrugged. "It's not our way. Your parents were far too liberal with the laws of our sect. I raised you correctly—"

"You sent her to the Common Guild on Raylia to get married?"

Abigail turned to Jesse with question in her narrowed eyes. "What's wrong?"

Pitney had the courtesy to look embarrassed. She still didn't understand.

"Darlin', The Common Guild of Raylia is the most infamous whore house in the solar system of Ksanthral. The puritan colony was put there expressly to rid the galaxy of the filth from sexual depravity freely flowing there. It's legendary across the solar system."

Abigail turned to Pitney and snarled, "You sent me across the galaxy and the other side of nowhere to a whore house?"

Chapter 13

"You misunderstood me, Abigail. I should have known you'd get it wrong. I sent you to the Saints of Aria sect on Raylia to be married to someone pious—"

"Which no longer matters," Jesse butted in. "She's my wife now and as such I want all the credits, which are hers, transferred to *my* account."

Pitney laughed. "What makes you think I'll do this?"

"Because of the additional information we discovered regarding certain transmissions to Raylia in the deep recesses of your files."

Pitney stilled. "I have no idea what you're talking about."

"Abigail isn't the first girl you sent to Raylia under false pretext. You preach of sending pilgrims with common goals to spread the faith and fight smut for the common good of your people. But in fact you have quiet a nice little business going. Don't you?"

Pitney shrugged and looked bored. "I'm sure I don't know what you're muttering about."

"We have copies of everything. Including a record of a certain communication device I've since learned is illegal for you to possess. The coordinates place it at your house, or rather Abigail's house, soon to be *my* house. We'll release the files to the Saints of Aria. Unless…" Jesse trailed off and grinned smugly.

"Unless I do what?"

Jesse produced another document protector. "Sign this and release the entire portion of Abigail's credits to my personal account. You can keep whatever you've managed to skim off and I'll even throw in the house. I'll give you the information we collected which you don't want anyone to see. Then I'll be on my way."

Pitney went from white faced to red. After several moments he leaned over and placed a thumbprint on the square transferring the credits to Jesse's account. He stood and asked, "What about Abigail?"

Jesse wrapped up the signed document up and laughed. "You can keep her."

The room went silent until it registered what he'd said.

Abigail reacted first. "What?"

Jesse turned to her with the sternest look he could muster. "Sorry, darlin', but I don't want a wife. You may remember I just got rid of one recently. I signed that proxy on Delocia because I knew I'd be able to figure a way to gain some credits. And I was right. You're beyond rich. Your guardian being an idiot with electronic accounting was like finding a treasure."

Abigail's stricken face dominated the room. "But what about us?"

Jesse smiled indulgently. "Us? There is no us, darlin'. I well and truly enjoyed you in my bed and I'll miss your home-made cooking, but honestly, I'm only interested in your substantial credit balance."

"You had carnal relations with her?" Pitney shouted.

Jesse laughed again. "Repeatedly."

Repugnance encompassed Pitney's florid face. He sneered. "Then take her with you. I never want to see her again."

"What am I going to do with her? Get rid of her yourself. You have the perfect business already established for it." Jesse moved towards the door.

"Jesse." Abigail's voice sounded well past the point of heartbroken.

"Hush." He held up one hand signaling that he didn't want to speak to her.

Pitney cleared his throat. "I'll hire you to take her to Raylia and drop her off with the Common Guild."

"What about the murder charge?" Tarik asked. "How will we get around that if we take her with us?"

"The murder charge isn't binding, but merely an inquiry. I'll simply tell the Segoha Defense officers she can be released."

"Doesn't matter," Jesse responded quickly. "Abigail is his problem now."

Pitney took a step forward. "Wait. I have a contact on Raylia. His name is Jorge Smith. He'll pave the way into the facility and give you a few credits since she's so young."

"Jorge Smith?" Jesse frowned. "*He* was your contact on Raylia?"

"Yes. Why? Do you know him?"

"Maybe." Jesse shrugged. "I know he's not taking on girls for the Common Guild any more."

"How do you know that?" Pitney practically growled.

"I've heard tell he's no longer in business. He met with foul play recently." Jesse's posture tightened as soon as the words left his mouth. *Damn it.* He shouldn't have spoken. He shouldn't have admitted his knowledge of Jorge Smith's unfortunate accident.

The recent stupidity of trying to rescue himself from Lola's financial claws reared its ugly head ready to take a big chomp out of his ass yet again.

"That's preposterous. I sent Abigail to him less than a month ago."

"Be that as it may, old Jorge met with an Infiltrator's Special bullet with his name on it. A fate he likely wasn't expecting."

"He's dead?" Pitney's shocked tone was sincere.

"No. But for your purposes he might as well be. I heard he was paralyzed and bed-ridden." Jesse glanced at Tarik who gave him a very telling and stern look. His crew knew where Jesse had gone on his recent trip to perform a contract and acquire the blood money from his "secret" patron for Lola's payoff. The hit had taken place on Raylia, and the payment had been made on one of Raylia's ten moons two days later.

Tarik wouldn't rat him out now or ever, but a conversation was likely coming between the two of them. He'd never shared his past with anyone in his crew with regard to his time as a prestigious member the Galactic Gunman. No one on his ship knew he'd once, and still, held an Infiltrator weapon. And they especially didn't know he still had that illegal weapon in his possession.

Jesse didn't relish a confession, but made a mental note to be prepared for a time when Tarik would certainly bring it up again.

Pitney leaned forward as if in an effort to convince him to take Abigail off of his hands. "That's inconvenient, however, I have no doubt some other man has stepped into Mr. Smith's role. It shouldn't be too difficult for you to pawn her off at the Common Guild with or without a contact."

"And you're going to pay me to make it further worth my while?"

Pitney's lips flattened. "Yes. I'll pay you."

"Are you sure you can have the murder charge dismissed? I don't want any trouble leaving the planet."

"There shouldn't be a murder charge. I never killed anyone." Abigail's angry gaze shot to Jesse.

"Be quiet," Pitney told her and closed his eyes a moment. "I'll take care of it. As I said, it isn't an official murder charge, just a suspicion that I whispered in the authorities ears to explain her absence from the planet so soon after Myron's death. I can take it away just as easily. Are we agreed? Will you take her to Raylia?"

Jesse sighed with extreme annoyance, "All right. But it's going to cost you, Mr. Pitney. Make a transfer for five hundred credits from your personal account and we'll call it a deal."

"Four hundred credits."

Jesse smiled. "Done." He nodded at Tarik who quickly grabbed one of Abigail's upper arms in a vise-tight grip. Jesse completed the transaction as Tarik pulled her now struggling body, toward the door.

"Wait! What about my Aunt Eugenia? Please. What will happen to her? Please, Jesse. You said she could come with us. You said you would rescue her."

Jesse barked at her in mirthless laughter. "I lied to you darlin'. I certainly don't want another passenger to deal with. You're going to be a handful as it is."

A low rumbling laughter came from Tarik. "You know, Captain, there are those who will pay huge amounts of credits for older women at the Common Guild on Raylia. Especially ones that aren't all used up after years of whoring."

Jesse paused and stroked his chin in thought. "You're right, Tarik." He turned back to Pitney. "We'll take her Aunt Eugenia, as well. A great deal for you, two for the price of one. Where is she?"

"No!" Abigail screamed and fought uselessly against Tarik's tight hold. "You wouldn't do that. You can't send her to that terrible place. The elder home is better."

Pitney caught Abigail's horrified gaze and a sinister smile slid across his mouth. "I'll release the old crone out of the elder house to your custody." Pitney pulled out a paper and stepped into the hall of the jail. He spoke to someone outside and stuck a head in. "Where do you want her sent?"

"Have her sent immediately to my ship, the *Dragonfly*, docked at bay five." Jesse smiled and decided this arrangement had worked out even better than he'd planned.

* * * *

Abigail was living through a nightmare of the worst variety because she was wide awake.

Pitney signed the documents to release her aunt as Abigail watched in dismay. How could she have been so wrong about Jesse? How could she have believed he cared for her? How could she have trusted him?

Jesse eased into Pitney's personal space and in a low lethal tone said, "It goes without saying that you shouldn't try to come after me or my ship. If you send anyone after me for retribution, I'll simply dispose of them and come after you myself. Are we clear?"

"Yes," Pitney grated out through clenched teeth.

"Just in case, I'll keep a few of the documents on your indiscretions as insurance."

Jesse exited the room without giving her a backward glance. Tarik pulled on her arm and led her in her husband's wake.

"*Beastulio*. I hate you," she spat out to Jesse's back as he exited the room. He paused momentarily and glanced over his shoulder at her vile curse, but continued walking out the door.

From behind her, Pitney laughed in a self-satisfied rumble. Abigail hated that he was happy about her new nightmare existence. Bound for an infamous whorehouse on Raylia with a man she'd fallen in love with, Abigail tried to stop shaking in fury over this turn of events.

The three of them made their way to the *Dragonfly* still docked at bay five.

They stopped by the Segoha defense area building for release paperwork and to confirm Pitney had transferred the credits. Jesse reached inside his coat pocket, retrieving a communication device. "Start the *Dragonfly* up, Tiger. We're leaving as soon as Abigail's aunt is on board."

Abigail heard Tiger answer, "She's already here, Captain."

"Excellent, put her in the brig and set a course for Raylia."

"Roger that, Captain. Into the brig she'll go." Tiger sounded jubilant. The whole crew was in on this travesty. Abigail felt so foolish, so utterly betrayed.

"Oh, and contact the Common Guild. Tell them I need to negotiate a contract for the two of them once we get underway."

"Yes, sir. Tiger out."

"I can't believe I ever trusted you. I can't believe I let you use my body. You are the most despicable man I've ever had the displeasure to deal with and far worse than Pitney."

"Am I?" Jesse turned around as Tarik tightened his grip on her arm hindering her escape. Where would she go? She had to hope there would be a chance on the way to Raylia. At least her aunt was out of the elder house, even if they were both on the way to a much worse destiny.

"Well, try not to let your anger show, darlin'. It's a long way to Raylia and I still expect you to warm my bed all the way there."

"Well, don't expect me to be as willing from now on." Tears of anger formed in her eyes and spilled down her cheeks.

Glancing around the room at all the Segoha defense members listening in with self-satisfied smirks, Abigail swallowed hard.

Jesse looked around at those pretending not to listen. "You're still my wife. Mine to order around at will as I read and understand the laws of your sect." He leaned in until the breath from his traitorous lips caressed hers. "I expect you'll do anything I demand all the way to Raylia so take care with your words or I'll punish you. I can always tie you to my bed and only let you up to cook my meals."

Tears fell heedlessly down her cheeks as they exited the building. Jesse led and Tarik followed, pushing her in front of him as he held tight to her upper arms. A group of defense officers followed them out as escort. She heard them snickering and whispering at the loud spectacle they made.

She shrieked at Jesse's back. "You made me fall in love with you only to betray me worse than Pitney ever did. There is nothing worse you can do to me than what you've already done."

Behind her, Tarik snorted.

Jesse stopped, turned, and stared at her a moment before seeming to realize they weren't alone. He looked around the Segoha dock at the defense men following them. "We'll just see about that, darlin'."

They entered the lower deck of the *Dragonfly*. Jesse turned and waved at the Segoha Defense men who'd escorted them all the way to the ship. As soon as the door shut completely to the Segoha dock, Tarik released her arms and backed away from her a step. Abigail heard him chuckle. She didn't find anything at all humorous about what had transpired on her home planet. If anything, it was far worse.

The doors locked behind her with a finality she wasn't ready to accept.

Jesse turned to her with a shocking and inappropriate grin in place on his handsome visage. Abigail launched herself at him with her hands aiming for his face. He grabbed her forearms before she could mark his face with her outstretched fingernails.

"I can't wait until we reach Raylia. As soon as I step off this ship I'll be free from you and your treacherous lies. At least as a whore with the Common Guild I'll know where I stand. You are a disappointment I'll regret for the rest of my life."

Tarik laughed. "Told you she'd fall for it. You should have warned her."

Jesse pierced her with a regretful look. "I couldn't warn her. She needed to believe it or Pitney would have seen through the farce and stopped me." Jesse lowered his face to hers. "That was an act for the benefit of your guardian, Abigail. If he thought you were the one with the credits, he would have found a way to hound you until the day you died.

"The Segoha defense contingent would have supported him and even allowed the use of the evil technology if it meant money in their pockets. Now they believe I legally have all the credits. Pitney won't come after me. And that means he also won't bother to come after you."

Abigail wrinkled her brows as another tear spilled on her cheek. "But you put my aunt in your brig."

"Darlin', I'm a transport captain. I don't have a brig. Your aunt is resting in my visitor's quarters."

"Oh." Her eyes welled up with fresh tears of embarrassment this time. Her mind raced with the new facts.

"I have successfully retrieved your credits, your freedom and your aunt from the elder house without blasting my way off of Segoha in a heated battle I wouldn't win. And you have all the credits you should have had when your parents died. At least once I transfer them out of my personal account. And I will, just as soon as you are set up somewhere. I promise."

"I see." She lowered her gaze from his. She was ashamed to have been so gullible to fall for his act. She'd shared her body and soul with him. She loved him. She'd then promptly failed the first test of loyalty. "Where will you take me?"

"Wherever you want to go. Although, I don't recommend Raylia or Delocia."

"I believed—" She raised her eyes to his blinking tears of shame.

"I know. I'm sorry it was necessary." His eyes did not seek her out.

He turned and pushed the button on the communication device. "Tiger? Get ready to blast off. I want us away this planet as fast as possible.

"Roger that, Captain. We'll be on our way in a few minutes."

Jesse glanced at the floor avoiding her gaze. She'd hurt him with her horrible words. She tried to think of something to say in the way of apology, but the lift they were on suddenly stopped. The doors opened to the hallway leading to the living area of the *Dragonfly*. The three of them departed without any words being said.

Jesse led the way through the doors to the common room as she walked silently behind him still trying to think of something to say.

"Abby, my love." Aunt Eugenia's squeal of delight greeted her.

Abigail turned in time to be enveloped in her aunt's arms. The scent of lemon verbena overwhelmed her and teardrops fell copiously. The tears she'd shed for not trusting Jesse were interpreted by tears of joy at their reunion. She lost track of Jesse in the wake of her aunt's chatter.

"Glory be, Abby. I'm very happily surprised to see you. I was afraid we'd never speak again in this lifetime. Pitney turned out to be the scoundrel we always thought he was. He had me ensconced at the elder house before that pitiful ship you were on lifted off from Segoha and took you away."

"I know. I'm glad you're safe, Auntie."

"This ship is wonderful. The folks here are so nice. Pru used to live on Segoha. Did you know that? I knew her great-grandmother once upon a time..."

Abigail let her aunt chatter on as she led them to the visitor's quarters. There was a suite of two bedrooms inside, each with its own separate bath and a common room separating them.

"Are you all right, Aunt Eugenia?" Abigail asked.

Aunt Eugenia smiled warmly. "I'll be fine, dear. Are *you* all right?"

Abigail shrugged. So much had happened so quickly that she hadn't had time to process it. Two months ago she wondered how to get out of an arranged marriage to an old man. Today she wondered what she'd do with the rest of her life if she couldn't have Jesse in it.

"It was my fault you were left to Pitney, you know," her aunt said quietly. "The Saints of Aria said I wasn't fit to raise you. They thought I was too flighty. Your parents never wanted Pitney in your life. I'm sorry I wasn't strong enough to stop it."

Abigail gave her aunt a hug. "It wasn't your fault. I'm delighted to know my parents wanted a different life for me."

Aunt Eugenia kissed her forehead and patted her back just like she'd always done. Abigail took strength in her embrace. She squeezed her Aunt Eugenia's ample waist. "I'm suddenly very tired. I think I'll go rest in the other bedroom. Will you be all right?"

Her aunt nodded. Abigail stepped into the extra visitor's quarter's bedroom. Jesse would never want her to grace his bed again since she'd been so hateful. She knew he wanted her to speak her mind, but she'd called him a *Beastulio* and she'd done so in public. It was an offense that was difficult to forgive. And worse, at the time she'd meant it with all the hatred in her sorely betrayed heart. She sniffed back relentless tears unable to stop crying.

Should she try to apologize for her hateful actions, yet again?

He was surely sick and tired of her lame and seemingly short termed, repentance. She tossed and turned on the visitor's room bed wishing she had the courage to march down the hallway to Jesse's room and attempt one more act of contrition.

Chapter 14

The knock on his door sent Jesse's lovesick heartbeat racing with hope. He strode over to his cabin door and snatched it open wishing to find his latest soon-to-be ex wife. Serial weddings were a habit he hoped to break very soon.

Tarik and not Abigail stood in the doorway. Jesse stiffened and tried to tell himself that he wasn't disappointed. But he was.

"What do *you* want?" He didn't mean to sound so pissed off. But he was.

"Before too much time gets away from us, I'd like to have a conversation with you, Jesse." Without an invitation, Tarik pushed Jesse aside and entered unbidden into his quarters.

"Come on in and make yourself at home." Jesse didn't hide the sarcasm in his tone.

The grunt Tarik issued likely substituted as a noncommittal response.

"What do you want to talk about?" Jesse knew *exactly* what Tarik wanted to discuss.

"I'd like to discuss Jorge Smith's unfortunate fate on the distant planet of Raylia and the weapon used to dispatch him to his new circumstances."

Jesse admired Tarik's blunt ability to get directly to the point on most occasions, but not today. "I decline to discuss that subject. What else would you like to talk about?"

"How about the ramifications of harboring an illegal Infiltrator revolver aboard this ship? If you're hiding criminal activities, I think the rest of us have a right to know."

Jesse shook his head. "No, you don't. I'm the captain of this vessel. If there's something you don't like, tough shit. Either keep your feelings to yourself or don't let the hatch door hit you in the ass on your way off of my ship."

Tarik was a big man. He took one step closer to Jesse. The thought occurred that he was about to get punched in the face for his snotty remarks, but Tarik suddenly threw his head back and laughed.

"What's so funny?"

"I always expect you to back down when I pretend to be hostile, but you never do. Makes me like you more."

Jesse rolled his eyes. "I'm glad you find me so fucking amusing. Is that all? I'm kinda busy right now."

Tarik glanced around. "Doing what? Your wife is still in the visitor's rooms with her aunt."

"I know where she is," Jesse growled.

"Back to my original subject. I don't care what you do on your ship as long as it doesn't have any impact on me or Pru. So all I'll say is this, don't make any mistakes with that gun. There are ways to trace those special bullets."

Jesse crossed his arms. "How do you know?"

"How do you think?" Tarik smiled. "We share a similar past profession, Jesse. I was a Galactic Gunman from the first day they issued badges."

"So did you give your weapon up to the melting pot?"

His dark brows furrowed. "What do you think?"

"I think if you have any illegal weapons stored on my ship that *I'm* the one who has a right to know."

Tarik shook his head and a long sigh erupted. "Tell me you have pre-issued blank template bullets and I'll leave you alone."

Jesse smiled. He didn't plan to tell Tarik what he wanted to know and it was just as likely Tarik wouldn't confess either, but having a former Gunman in his ranks made Jesse feel better.

"I'm not going to confirm or deny anything. But I will say this, only an idiot would use traceable bullets on an illegal weapon." Jesse fixed his gaze on Tarik's stern visage. "I hope that if you're harboring an illegal weapon aboard this ship you have the sense to keep it in a radar shielded gun container."

"Only a moron would keep an Infiltrator revolver in a standard gun box."

"Touché." The hint of amusement on Tarik's face made Jesse relax. Tarik walked past him to the door. "I'm glad we had this talk, Jesse."

"Whatever." Jesse's focus went back to the lack of Abigail being in his room.

Tarik paused in the doorway and turned back. "Pru thinks you should go tell your wife how you feel about her and make up."

"I don't need any advice on my love life," Jesse huffed and slammed the cabin door on Tarik's gut rolling laughter.

* * * *

Restful sleep escaped Abigail through the night as tears soaked her pillow. Jesse must hate her. Troubling dreams of dying alone calling out to Jesse in vain cluttered her rest.

She woke hours later, eyes aching, heart bitter from her own making and stomach rumbling. She glanced at the automatic time piece on the wall and realized she'd slept through dinner by six hours.

Dressing in the clothing provided in the visitor's suite, she prepared to go to the galley. The shirt and slacks she put on were slightly bigger than her size, but serviceable. She felt odd not to have her dress on, but these clothes were so much more comfortable.

Abigail went to the common room and did what she always did when a problem plagued her conscious. She cooked.

An hour later and seated before several baked goods on the table, a hand on her shoulder made her jump.

"Sorry, darlin'. I didn't mean to startle you." Jesse stood behind her. He looked haggard. "I missed you last night."

"Did you? I wonder why."

A warm smile lit his face. "You're soft to sleep next to and well, I guess I've grown accustom to you being there."

"I thought you were furious. I deserve your wrath for all the things I said."

"I was never mad at you, Abigail." He shrugged. "I would have fetched you last night and told you, but I figured you'd want to spend some time with your aunt and catch up."

She nodded and gave voice to what he already knew. "I stayed with her in the visitor's quarters." Unable to think of what to do next or what to say, Abigail remained quiet.

He stared at her pensively, sat down beside her and also said nothing further.

She straightened her spine and announced, "I made breakfast."

Elbows resting on the table, Jesse smiled. "I see. Thank you."

"You really hate me, don't you? I called you a vile name in public when you only tried to rescue me again. I've been a terrible wife."

Jesse inhaled deeply and snaked an arm around her waist. He pulled her to his side. "No. I miss you, darlin'. You aren't a bad wife. Not at all. Given the same circumstances, I would have called me a vile name, too. Plus, I enjoyed seeing that rebellious streak flare out when we were on Segoha."

Abigail laughed. "You're the only man I've ever known who enjoys my disobedience."

Jesse gave her a look she couldn't identify. "I wish things had been different."

"Different?"

Jesse caught her gaze with one of longing. "You know, that we'd met under different circumstances."

"I don't understand. What's wrong with the way we met, aside from the murder charge and the unexpected marriage?" She smiled and leaned closer.

He grinned but soon sobered. "Darlin', I think you deserve a chance to do what you want without a husband or a guardian directing you. Now with the credits you have, you can do anything you want to, go anywhere in the galaxy you choose to visit." He held up another document protector much like the one her proxy for a fake Raylia marriage to a flesh peddler with the Common Guild.

Jesse had saved her from a fate worse than death by signing those papers. He'd rescued her aunt and saved her from the abuse at the elder house. "I'll sign an annulment and transfer your funds to wherever you end up residing."

"You deserve a better wife. But I do love you. I want you to know that I always will no matter where I end up. I'll always be grateful to you for everything you've done."

Jesse leaned in close and kissed her forehead tenderly. "I never wanted a wife, but if I did I'd choose you in the split second of a heartbeat."

"You would?"

"Yep."

Abigail melted into his body and shared what was on her mind. "I was thinking about signing on to the *Dragonfly* as your cook. Would you give me a job, Captain?"

His eyes smoldered with passion. "The only job I want you for is wife. I love you, too. I think I have since I saw you storm into the Delocia Allied Supply Hut anger flashing in your gorgeous sea green eyes."

She threw her arms around his neck. "I've loved you since you told me I didn't have to sleep with you to get the part I didn't really need for Dooley's ship. It was very honorable."

"Well, maybe honorable but also the most foolish thing I ever said, because I didn't mean it. I wanted to sleep with you more than I wanted to breathe. Your freckles are irresistible." He kissed her nose. His lips lowered to hover over hers a breath away from kissing her.

"Can we eat yet?" Tiger's impatient voice sounded from the open doorway to the common room. "I'm hungry and are those griddle cakes with honey flower syrup?"

"Leave them be. They love each other." Pru poked him in the ribs. "Your stomach can wait a few more minutes."

The entire crew including her aunt Eugenia hovered in and around the doorway to the common room, watching their embrace.

"He's very handsome, Abby. I think you should keep him." Aunt Eugenia had a grin wreathing her face.

Jesse huffed. "Come on in. I can see we won't get any peace until Tiger's stomach is satisfied."

"Ask her to stay married to you," Pru said in a loud whisper. "You'll never find anyone else willing to put up with you."

Jesse looked at the ceiling as if gathering strength and then focused his passionate gaze on her. "Will you please stay married to me, Abigail?"

She grinned. "Yes, as long as you love me."

"I do love you." He kissed her lips and ignored his crew now crowding around them to sample the food she'd prepared.

Epilogue

"Are you sure you aren't jealous when we do this?" Abigail asked for the third time since they'd entered the cube tonight.

"Yes, darlin', I'm sure I don't get jealous. It's just make believe." Jesse put his hand on the base of her spine and propelled her further inside.

"Do you want other women?"

"No. I only want you." Jesse grinned and kissed the end of her pert nose. Holding up the remote operating device, he whispered, "We don't have to do this if you don't want to—"

Abigail broke in. "Oh, I want to, I just worry that it's unfair."

"It's not, I promise. My fantasy is watching you enjoy sexual pleasure." He stood in front of the VR cube settings panel. "Now would you like Hector, Clive or Sven tonight?"

"Clive." Her seductive whispered response lit his libido on fire. Her eyes slid shut and the anticipation on her face pinched him low in the belly. He loved this woman more than his own life.

Being in virtual realm of the cube and watching other men pleasure her was likely the most carnal and satisfying of practices in their marriage. He didn't need any other women to distract his attention from his darling Abigail. One day she'd understand and until then she'd worry and he would reaffirm and reassure her that their time together in "the cube" held many of his best memories.

Jesse pushed a button and then pocked the remote. The scene change melted around them with amazing clarity. When Abigail opened her eyes, they stood at the base of the stone veranda leading to the mountain retreat on Selinasta where they'd honeymooned for two weeks last year. Selinasta, a rare tropical atmosphere in the Ksanthral system, was a very expensive trip outside of the VR cube. Inside, it was the perfect setting to reenact memories.

"I love this place," she whispered and took a step forward.

"Me too."

Clive waited for them at the top of the stairs, his ice blue eyes beckoning Abigail forward with promises of giddy satisfaction to come. Jesse put a hand on her ass and followed her up the wide staircase until she stood before their "playmate" for this evening.

"Hi, Clive."

"Hello, Abigail. I've missed you." Clive took her hand and kissed each of the fingers he held. "Shall we start with a drink? I've made up some frosty blue pineapple flavored beverages for us to cool off with as a start to our evening. Would you like one?"

"Yes."

Clive leaned forward and kissed her mouth once before turning to pour a blue liquid into the tall chill-frosted champagne flute. Jesse pressed a kiss to a sensitive spot on the back of her neck as Clive handed her the drink.

Abigail accepted the glass and took a long sip. Clive inched closer, palmed each of her breasts and rubbed gently through the skimpy shirt she wore. She downed the drink and moaned as Jesse slid his hands to her hips to hold her in place. He aligned his cock at the base of her spine and pushed his hips forward with tender care.

Sandwiched between them, Abigail sighed as her shoulder blades melted against Jesse's chest. Clive kissed her mouth and pulled the straps of her dress over each shoulder to reveal her taut nipples. He kissed his way down until he latched his lips around one peak.

Abigail arched to give Clive better access to her breasts. Jesse watched over one lovely shoulder with lust at watching his wife pleasured. He pressed his lips to her neck and nibbled the sensitive spot she had there.

Clive got on his knees and lifted her skirt in the front, ducking his head beneath. Abigail moaned and Jesse figured he'd started licking her clit already.

Jesse trailed kisses down her bare back to one shoulder blade. He lifted her long skirt and discovered she wasn't wearing anything beneath it. Another surge of lust coated his insides and he squeezed her naked thighs once to show his appreciation. "I see you've decided to embrace your rebelliousness tonight, darlin'. Good for you. I love it when you do that."

"Only for you, Jesse."

Loosening his fly, Jesse released his cock and nudged it between her legs. Clive's tongue slid briefly across his shaft as he sunk his cock as deeply as it would go into Abigail's pussy. Heaven waited for him there. As Jesse began thrusting over and over into her hot body, Abigail made the most decadent sounding noises.

Having Clive's tongue lick his shaft at every other thrust added a surprising component he hadn't expected to enjoy. Any tongue is good tongue, he decided and picked up the rhythm of his thrusts until he didn't feel anything except the explosion of pleasure when his tip of his dick hit Abigail's womb.

Her back arched against his chest and her soft sigh of pleasure sent a virulent and powerful surge of love to his soul. He loved this woman with all his heart. He stopped thrusting long enough to kiss and nibble the back of her neck until she begged, "Please, Jesse, don't stop."

Jesse reached around and grabbed a handful of her luscious breast, pierced her pussy with his cock deeper than he'd ever thought he could go and listened as she shrieked his name. She climaxed and the ripples of her orgasm clamped his cock in wondrous pressure. Clive stood and stepped away as he was programmed to do. Abigail only wanted Jesse's presence when she recovered from her orgasms. Three strokes later Jesse came in a rush of sensation so powerful, he was amazed he remained conscious.

"I love you, Jesse," she whispered and swayed on her feet.

"I love you, too, darlin', but we need to find a bed." Jesse, still intimately connected, took a wobbly step to the right and pulled her onto a large, low bed surrounded on the other three sides by gauzy curtains. She turned in his arms and kissed his mouth with a rebellious flare she knew he loved.

"I know I've said it before, but I love the VR cube."

Jesse laughed. "I know you do, and in the spirit of variety, I have an idea for a sexy VR program to try next time."

She trailed fingertips along his collarbone. "What is it?"

"How about we reenact the first time we met at the Allied Supply Hut? Only this time I'll come around the counter and have my wicked way with you before we leave the premises without bothering to take any parts."

She giggled against his chest and nodded. "I'd be willing to try it if you also create an additional program to have your wicked way with me in the Delocia jail house before rescuing me."

"Ah, my rebellious little wife wants some roll play and a conjugal prison visit, huh? Great idea." Jesse kissed Abigail and knew she was the only woman he'd ever want. "Then we'll trade places. I'll pretend to be a rogue criminal and you can be 'my' special visitor."

"You are a rogue. You don't have to pretend."

"Only for you, darlin'."

THE END

ABOUT THE AUTHOR

Lara Santiago is the bestselling author of over twelve books. She's an Ecataromance award winner, a 2007 Passionate Plume finalist for *The Lawman's Wife*, and has garnered a coveted four and half stars from Romantic Times Book Reviews for her novel, *The Blonde Bomb Tech*.

From her futuristic novels to her contemporary romantic suspense, she's known for her independent heroines and those compelling alpha males we all adore.

After turning in her twelfth manuscript, she came to the realization that this writing gig might just work out after all. She continues to dream up stories, keeping no less than ten story ideas circulating at any given time.

Enjoy Excerpts from Menagerie

Available at SirenPublishing.com

[Siren Ménage Amour #9: Erotic Sci-fi Romance, Multiple Sex Partners, Sharing]

What's a girl to do with five hot guys who need her for their sexual survival? Create a weekly schedule.

Accidentally transported to an alien spaceship, Valerie Thornhill inadvertently volunteers to be a virtual sex slave for five men.

A shortage of females and her blatant curiosity aboard the alien vessel conspire and set fate in motion. The fact that the five are sexy and attractive is helpful when she learns the term of service is three years.

Forbidden to show favoritism within her unusual household for the duration of the long trip, Valerie still can't help falling in love with the most intriguing one of her male harem. The fact that she is apprehensive about his demeanor and overall size only heightens her desire for him.

When the aliens discover Valerie's indiscretion, the ultimate price for her desire may jeopardize the return trip to Earth for all of them.

STORY EXCERPT

"...is why the men here need sex." An unrecognized voice echoed in Valerie's sluggish brain.

Join the club, she thought, rousing further. She opened her eyes and realized she was sitting in a very uncomfortable chair.

"Therefore, after the gauntlet arena selection, you will be required to have sex with each one of the men in your selected group at least once every two months so that they won't die a painful death," the blue alien standing before her said in a stern tone.

Valerie was no longer face down in the dirt. She was no longer outdoors. Lifting her head slowly, she quickly realized she was also no longer alone. Half slumped in a hard metal chair, she straightened and stretched the kinks out of her back. After several satisfying pops, she resisted the urge to yawn.

Where am I?

Looking first to her right, she noticed fifteen or so other shell-shocked-looking women in various stages of dress. To her left was much the same view. There was one poor soul wearing only a bra and panties. But another was in a full fledged business suit complete with patterned pantyhose and stilettos. The others in the room looked like they'd been pulled from backstage at a play between acts.

Valerie looked down at her boring gray sweats. At least she wasn't in her underwear like half the women in the room.

The blue alien looked like a body builder that had been dipped in cerulean paint. He cleared his throat and all the women in the room sent their gaze forward. No one in the room spoke.

The grimace forming on his face wasn't attractive and bordered on hostile. He stared as if he was waiting for something from them. Valerie had no idea what it could be and resisted the urge to yawn, certain it wasn't the response he searched for. She wished she hadn't missed the first part of what he'd said.

"Don't any of you have questions?" he asked. "I usually get a lot of questions."

Valerie raised her hand. The blue alien man's expression softened. He pointed at her and gestured that she stand.

She sighed deeply and stood. Over a sea of heads seated in the several rows of chairs in front of her, Valerie fixed her gaze on the strange blue man waiting with eyebrows lifted for her question.

"What was your name again?"

He stiffened. "You may call me, Blue. What is your question? Or was that it?"

Valerie paused at his name. His skin was blue and his name was Blue? Whatever.

"We haven't got all day," he remarked and glanced at his clipboard thing.

"You want me to do what with a group of strange men?"

He sent a piercing stare through her, crossed his substantial arms over his chest and the hostile expression returned. "Haven't you been listening?"

Blue, the alien with the Smurf-blue skin, looked like he'd fallen into a vat of sapphire dye and soaked for awhile. Maybe that's why he was so grumpy. His hair was dark brown along with his thick eyebrows and his eyes were also brown. He wore snug pants and no shirt.

"Well, sure, to part of it, but." she trailed off and sat back down.

Was she dreaming? If so, wouldn't she be the one in her underwear being called to task in the classroom?

"Have any of you been listening?" he railed and sent another stern gaze drilling to several of the other women.

No one else said a word. Perhaps they were all as confused as she was.

Valerie decided that this was the single most vivid dream she'd ever had, and the strangest. She felt like she'd come into the middle of a movie. Only she didn't remember how she got here or where she'd been before being seated at the back of the class. Someone else must have put her here, because if she'd seated herself, she would have been in the front row. Definitely a dream.

She sent her gaze forward again. Blue's expression hadn't changed from annoyance. A couple of phrases brushed her memory. Gauntlet arena with groups of men and have sex with each of them. If she'd remembered correctly.

Yeah. Like that would really happen. She barely knew what to do with one man let alone a group of them. The rest of the women seated around her seemed even less enthusiastic.

"Don't any of you have anything to say?"

No one responded.

The few women standing along the edges of the room, possibly due to the inadequate seating, seemed equally shocked into speechlessness by Blue's words. Perhaps it was a group dream.

Blue sighed deeply, as if he were dealing with children who were too ignorant to comprehend his words. "Don't you understand? There are never enough women to go around when you are brought here, so the men have to share. They suffer if they have to go without sex for that long in this environment. Do you want them to suffer?" He looked around the room, making eye contact with several of the attendees. "Well, do you?"

Like sheep afraid to stand up for themselves, they all began to shake their heads. Valerie didn't respond. She didn't particularly care about the suffering of strange horny men. It was a stupid dream, and therefore no participation was required.

"Now, we haven't much time, as we are running behind schedule. I don't have time to repeat myself. Therefore, we'll take you through orientation quickly and then bring you right to the beginner's gauntlet arena. It's a little quieter than the advanced one. Hopefully you can learn what you need to know along the way."

A woman to Valerie's right, who'd obviously been in the middle of putting make-up on and dressed completely in beige, raised her hand. "How many men are in a group?"

Blue nodded and the frown disappeared as if he'd finally heard a worthy question. "It varies. Never more than seven and no less than four. The average is five."

Valerie looked down at her gray jogging suit, wishing she'd managed to conjure up a nicer outfit for this dream. If she were about to meet men, a sweat suit wasn't exactly the most flattering clothing she could have worn.

Blue was talking again, but Valerie missed it due to her perusal of the unusual fashion statements being made around her. What did her clothing say about her? Was she an exercise geek? She sincerely hoped not.

The nebulous feeling in her brain wouldn't allow her to remember specifics of her life. She guessed it wasn't really important in the dream world.

".come along now to the next station and all the important facts will be explained in greater detail. You can make your decision then. Stay together. Don't wander off."

Blue headed towards the only door in the room and the other women followed, one after the other, until the room emptied.

Valerie ended up at the end of the line with one of the business-suited ladies directly ahead of her. She followed along down a narrow white hallway, looking all around for a clue as to where she might be. The walls seemed to be constructed of white panels with lights hidden inside. Didn't you usually dream about places that were familiar? Apparently not, because this place was totally alien.

Up ahead on the right, a panel had dislodged as if the wall had been hastily constructed. Through the gap, Valerie could see another hallway and she slowed to peek through. She lost sight of the business suit she was following to wrestle the panel open further.

After a little effort she was through the narrow space and into a much wider hallway. The color of the lights in this hall were varying hues of aqua. She liked this hallway much better. The color was more soothing.

Valerie chose to walk to the left because the hall was longer in that direction, and seemed to go farther. After walking for several minutes, she heard voices. She rounded a corner and plowed into someone.

A tall, male someone.

"I'm sorry. I didn't see you," said a totally luscious, deep male voice over her head. There was another man standing next to him, but Valerie couldn't tear herself away to get a look. The man she'd run into felt too good.

"I don't mind." Valerie grabbed his arms and laid her forehead on his chest. He smelled delicious. Taking a deep breath, she tilted her head up to check out his face. Wide shoulders led to a square jaw and he had a cleft in his chin, too. Focusing in on his vivid, saltwater-blue eyes last of all, she noted that he was completely gorgeous.

Valerie had read somewhere that dreams were thought to be the brain's way of cataloging information gathered during each day of the dreamer's life. She must have seen this hunk at the park or something and filed him away for later dreaming. He'd been worth the wait. Now in this dream, she could do anything that she wanted to with him.

Plus, she had the benefit of a better personality. In dreams she was always funnier, smarter and definitely prettier.

A bemused smile greeted her as she stared. He gripped her shoulders, squeezing gently. "Are you on your way to the gauntlet arena?"

Valerie scrunched her eyebrows. Hadn't that blue alien guy said something about an arena and a gauntlet?

"Is that where you're going?" she asked.

He nodded. "That's where I'm headed."

"Me too. Maybe we could walk together." She was prepared to say anything to keep this guy interested.

He exchanged amused glances with the man standing next to him and asked, "Are you spoken for yet?"

"I don't think so. How would I know for sure?"

"Have you selected any man from the gauntlet arena?"

"No." Valerie frowned. "What's that gauntlet arena thing again?" Better to get her answers from this hunk than a hostile blue alien.

He narrowed his eyes, then explained. "The gauntlet arena is a large room filled with men seeking a partner. When you enter and walk down the gauntlet aisle, the interested men will step forward and try to get your attention." He looked her up and down. "I expect you'll garner a lot of attention."

"Why?" His interested appraisal brought a grin to her lips. In her non-dream life she seldom rated a single look of interest from the men she came into contact with on a day-to-day basis. Attractive men like the man before her never saw her at all.

He smiled in return. "Well, first of all, you're a blonde. It's rare in this place, for some unexplained reason. And second of all," his eyes ran down her body with definite interest once again, "you aren't frighteningly skinny like the majority of the women here."

Valerie frowned and looked down at her crappy jogging suit. And while she'd always dreamed of being frighteningly skinny, she'd also always considered herself pleasingly plump. "Does that mean you think I'm fat?"

His eyes widened with panic. "No. Of course not. I meant absolutely no insult. It's just that the slightly curvier women are, well, more kindhearted in this place." He leaned in and whispered confidentially, "The bony, skinny ones are mean. It's not their fault. It has something to do with the alien vortex process when they're brought aboard."

Alien vortex process? Valerie drilled a look into his beautiful eyes, trying to understand. "How are the skinny chicks mean to you? What do they do?"

He shrugged. "It's their temperament, I guess. They go out of their way to aggravate all around them and especially men, but only after they've selected a group. By then it's too late. The new men here always go for the skinny, mean ones and subsequently they're stuck. Those women with a little meat on their bones are always selected first by the seasoned men here."

Valerie nodded, but didn't quite believe what he said. Her slightly hazy memory, which seemed to fade with each passing moment, recalled an incident very recently where a man she was with had suggested that she should go on a diet.

Even now the feeling of shame washed down her insides in a burning, hurtful rush. She shook her head to dissolve the remembered sting and lifted her eyes to his face. This was her dream, after all. She would control it and she most assuredly didn't want to think about diets.

This man's seductive gaze drilled through to her soul. His face reflected an expression suggesting that he liked what he saw in the deep, dark recesses of her mind.

"The men who have been here a while understand that principle, anyway, and I certainly do." His eyes traveled appreciatively down the rounded figure hidden by the boring jogging suit. "Yep, they're going to love you, all right."

Valerie nodded, released him and brushed her hands down her blah gray jogging shirt, which probably didn't enhance her round body in the least. "So after the interested men select me, then what?"

His gaze narrowed. "Then you select the one man you like best out of those who are interested and he takes you to meet his group."

"Oh yeah, the group. They mentioned the groups when I first got here. How many men are in your group?"

"Five."

Valerie nodded and smiled. "I hear that's the average."

"I guess."

"Then what?"

His eyebrows lifted. "Then if all of us agree you're the one for us, we seal the deal."

Sex? Did 'seal the deal' in this dream mean sex? Of course it did. It was her dream. It could mean whatever she wanted.

Valerie studied the man before her. He had a nice face. A patient face. He was tall and his wavy strawberry-blond hair and general body build reminded her of an Iowa farm boy. He perhaps also had a touch of Irish in his blood. Sexy, as far as she was concerned.

Valerie wanted to ensure she could find this man again. "What's your name?"

"You can call me Hauser."

"I'm Valerie." She reached out and touched his shoulder. She squeezed it. The muscle in his arm was solid, not like in her usual dreams, when you reached for something that you wanted and it vaporized.

He laughed nervously. "Are you sure you're okay, Valerie?"

"So can I just pick you? And you would be one of the men I spent time with here in this place?" She glanced around the sterile hallways where they stood as if someone might witness her molesting his shoulder with prurient intent.

His eyes widened and he looked over at his friend. The other man shook his head. Hauser chuckled and said, "I believe we have to make our selections in the gauntlet arena for it to count."

"Okay. Let's go there. I'd like to choose you. Is that okay?" Valerie ran her hand from his muscled chest to his fine flat abs. He made a sound somewhere between a grunt and a surprised growl. "Will you step up at the gauntlet arena so I can choose you?"

"Yes. I believe I will."

"Excellent." Valerie sighed. She knew she'd wake up before anything 'good' happened, but planned to enjoy this dream for as long as it lasted.

Hauser's smile dissolved and his expression hardened. "You understand what the five of us in our group want, right?"

She laughed. "Yes. You all want sex. I get it."

Hauser exchanged a knowing smile with his friend, who sent his gaze to the ceiling as if in disbelief. Perhaps he was looking for a partner too. The man who accompanied Hauser was attractive in a long-haired, rebel guy sort of way, but Valerie much preferred Hauser.

The three of them strolled down the blue-lit hallway. After two or three turns that completely made her lost, she noticed they now moved towards a group of people. There were several of the painted aliens dressed just like the first alien guy, only these two had green skin and blond hair.

Approaching slowly, Valerie saw that they stood outside a set of over-tall wooden double doors. A line of girls waited for entrance, and each time the door opened to admit one, a rousing cheer went up, cut off only by the door closing.

"So let me get this straight. I wait in line while you go inside. Then when it's my turn to go inside, I walk down the gauntlet, they cheer and then you'll come and get me."

"For the most part, yes, that's right. Keep walking as far as you can, I'll be towards the end of the gauntlet row. They'll be lining the ropes on either side. Sometimes it gets a little crowded by the time you get to the end, but I'll grab your wrist when you get close enough to me. If you still want to be with my group, just touch my skin anywhere. When the crowd clears, declare that you've chosen me."

She reached out and stroked her hand down his arm. "Should I yell out your name?"

Hauser shook his head. "Probably not. We shouldn't have met ahead of time. Some of the other men might complain that I took unfair advantage." He winked.

Mesmerized by his wink, Valerie finally answered, "Oh. Okay."

They were within shouting distance of the group waiting outside the tall doors, but no one had looked up to see them approaching yet. Hauser slowed his stride. "May I ask you a question?"

"Sure."

"If I select you as the mate for my group, how often will you allow sex for each of us?"

Valerie shrugged. "I don't know. What's the average for that sort of thing?" She expected to wake up before any actual sex took place, but she played along.

"The Others think that once every other month is enough."

"The Others?"

"That's what we call the multicolored aliens here."

Nodding, she asked, "And sex every other month isn't enough?"

"I've been here for almost two months already. I'm starting to get shaky. I hear at three months I'll want to die."

Valerie sympathized. She didn't want him to suffer for a second. Glancing back at the hallway they'd just come from, she wondered if she could talk him into a quickie in some remote closet. Just looking at him made her want to climb up his body, licking all the way. Given all the rules they seemed to have, she imagined that wouldn't happen. They probably had rules against closets and any licking taking place inside them.

"Hmm. Well, how about twice a month for each guy. What's that, ten times for me each month? I could do that, easy." Besides, it was a dream. Not like she would ever get to have any real sex with this gorgeous guy anyway. She would be on the verge of ecstasy, about to experience multiple orgasmic delights, and then her alarm clock would shrilly ring before the first ripple of climax hit her unsatisfied body.

That was the way her dreams always worked, frustratingly enough.

His eyes widened. "That would be very generous of you."

Valerie shrugged. "If they all look like you, it will be my pleasure." She suspected that even if the others looked like Quasimodo, the elephant man, king of the lepers and Satan, Hauser would still be worth it all on his own. He was a walking advertisement for the kind of insatiable sex appeal she'd only dreamed about. The kind of immediate attraction she'd waited for in her awake life. Could she drag Hauser back through this fabulous dream to her awake life? Likely not.

Hauser winked at her and separated himself before anyone noticed they'd walked down the hall together. He entered a smaller door next to the double doors where all the women in line entered one at a time.

Stepping up to the last woman in the long line, Valerie studied the other females while she waited for her turn. They'd obviously changed clothes. Many were attired in fancy dresses, sported freshly coiffed hair and wore makeup. The majority of them were frighteningly skinny, as Hauser had mentioned.

Valerie looked down at her sweat outfit and suddenly felt sort of foolish. Her hair was pulled away from her face and secured with a gray scrunchy, which matched her equally boring gray cotton jogging suit.

Over her shoulder, she noticed a fresh batch of four women, also dressed up in very fancy clothing, approach to stand in line behind her. She probably should have gone with the initial group to change, but she guessed it didn't matter. Valerie had a guy lined up and Hauser hadn't cared about her clothes. Undoubtedly, sex was more important than fashion from a male perspective. Suddenly, a disturbing thought occurred to her and she hoped Hauser hadn't been teasing her. It wouldn't be the first time a man had stood her up.

The gauntlet arena door opened and another exuberant cheer sounded as the woman in line directly ahead of Valerie disappeared through the tall entryway. She took a long step forward and into the attention of the new alien guy. He glanced up and down her body a few times as if with curiosity. His gaze finally landed on her face with an expression that said although he found her attire completely inappropriate, he didn't want to argue over it or stop the speed of the line to question her.

She broke the ice by speaking before he changed his mind and expressed disapproval of her clothing. "Let me guess, your name is Aqua."

"Correct." One light-blond eyebrow on his aqua-painted face lifted. "Are you ready to make your selection in the gauntlet arena?"

Valerie answered with a hesitant, "Yes," even as unease slid through her veins. Hauser had seemed very interested. She closed her eyes and sent up a little prayer that he wasn't lying about wanting her.

"When I open the door, make your way down the roped off areas. Look for those men you find appealing. Touch the skin of the one you want with your open hand and further instructions will follow."

"Right." Valerie nodded and shrugged as though she'd done this a hundred times before.

Without a further word, Aqua opened the door and ushered her through. Valerie was unprepared for the sheer volume of men in attendance. There must have been hundreds of them and another rousing cheer went up when she crossed the threshold into the large darkened room. She took two steps inside, and the door closed solidly behind her.

ADULT EXCERPT

"After you."

Valerie took a deep, silent breath and entered the room. Much like the room she'd originally met all of her men in, there was a sofa, two chairs and table in an arrangement, but beyond the entry was an open set of double glass doors leading to her perception of a fantasy bedroom.

What looked like miles of white gauzy fabric was artfully draped and swirled over a huge canopied, four-poster bed that was also covered in yards of white linen.

"Wow," she whispered. "Nice room. Like out of a fairy tale."

Hauser's hands landed on her shoulders. "Does it relax you enough for what's about to happen between us?"

Valerie turned to face a smiling Hauser as heat rose to her cheeks. "I'm not sure."

"Well, why don't we start with a kiss and see where that leads us." Hauser gently slipped his hands through her hair to cup her head. He leaned in for a kiss in the next second and the utter pleasure of his skillful tongue was enough to make her forget absolutely everything else.

He cradled her face with one hand as the other slid around her back to clench her solidly against his body.

It was no secret why they were here. Hauser hadn't had sex for a long time and she was here to relieve his discomfort. That was her job. Her primary purpose in this alternate reality.

Hauser's tongue brushed tenderly against hers and a tendril of desire unwound in her body. A moan escaped. He squeezed her tighter as more moaning ensued from her throat. Her vocal response prompted his hand to blaze a trail down her spine on a mission to massage her ass. His thickening cock pulsed between them, sending a shower of sensation and moisture between her legs.

The dress she wore was silk and she hadn't bothered to put any underwear on beneath it. Hauser broke the kiss to dip his hand beneath the hem at her knees. His light stroke skimmed up the outside of her thigh. When he discovered her lack of undergarments, he growled and thrust his hips forward.

He pulled away far enough to catch her eye and say, "My, aren't you just full of surprises."

"One or two." She pulled his head down for another sultry kiss.

His cock, huge and hard, pressed firmly into her stomach as a shudder rippled down his body. He squeezed her bare butt cheek once before sliding clever fingers between her legs. Two long fingers thrust inside her wet slit before she could protest. Not that she would have, but his intimate touch was a little shocking.

Her Swiss-cheese memory gave her little in the way of a foundation from her previous sexual experience. Given that every touch from his fingers seemed alien and overwhelming, she decided that she might be fairly inexperienced. His fingers slid in and out of her slick entrance easily and the feeling, while deliciously decadent, also felt incredibly naughty.

His thumb rubbed across her sensitive clit and she jumped backwards in surprise, breaking not only the kiss, but the intimate connection.

Panting, Hauser asked, "What's wrong?"

"I.um.nothing. I'm.just not used to.you know." She ended her stuttering sentence with a whisper.

The rate of his breathing said he was still trying to get it under control. "No. Tell me."

"I don't remember much about my life on Earth, but I get the feeling that I'm not very experienced.sexually. What you're doing to me.seems very unexpected.and naughty."

He laughed. "That's okay. I think naughty pretty much describes this whole scenario. But don't worry, I'll teach you everything you need to know."

Valerie nodded. "Okay." She took a deep breath and released it.

"God, you're sexy." He grabbed her shoulder with one hand, hugged her close and planted his lips sensually across her mouth, teasing her lips open with his tongue.

He danced her backwards slowly, through the double glass doors and into the bedroom. His tongue dipped and swirled inside her mouth, dueling with hers to a tempo only he could hear. Valerie slung her arms around his neck to hold on as they traveled. The thick ridge of his cock ground into her belly and aroused speculation regarding his size. She now knew he was huge and a ripple of arousal trickled down her body in anticipation as her core throbbed in readiness for him.

Once next to the bed, he yanked the zipper of her dress from neck to ass in one smooth, loud zip and a blast of cool air brushed her bare back. Hauser separated them enough to pull the pink dress off of her body. She was completely naked underneath.

She boldly grabbed his cock, which pulsed against her belly, and squeezed. He was indeed huge.

"Jesus, that feels incredible." Hauser gave her a salacious grin and quickly pulled his clothing off until he, too, was completely naked. He reached past her and pulled the comforter down, exposing the sheets. As he straightened, he latched his lips onto her breast, sucking one lucky nipple into the depths of his warm mouth.

Valerie slid her hands to his face to hold him in place as the most acute pleasure rode wildly inside her. He suckled and a delightful zing shot straight to her clit and a gush flooded the core of her pussy. Hauser didn't linger, but soon kissed a path from breast to mouth and drove his tongue languidly inside her mouth as he pulled her snugly against his pulsing erection. She nudged him with her hips and he clutched her even tighter.

"You feel so good, Valerie," he murmured against her cheek. "I don't think I can last too much longer."

"You don't have to. Take me to bed. I don't want you to suffer anymore."

"Trust me, I'm not suffering at all." He latched his mouth to hers.

Enjoy an Excerpt from
Sex or Suffer: Dark Colony 1

Available at SirenPublishing.com

[Siren Menage Amour 23: Erotic Sci-Fi, Multiple Sex Partner Romance]

Devastated to discover she harbors the SOS virus, medical researcher, Dr. Penelope Drake hires Captain Gray Wyckoff to take her across the galaxy to the cure on Parsec Five. As Penelope fights for a permanent remedy to cure this monstrous disease, the deplorable question in her mind repeats: How did she contract the virus in the first place?

Captain Gray Wyckoff burns every bridge he's ever built to get Penelope there, only to find she can't deliver the payment she's promised. Serving as her temporary sexual cure along the way only adds to his feelings of betrayal. He thought he loved her. Now he's not sure he can forgive her. Love her? Leave her? The choice between sex or suffering has never been so hard to make.

Especially when he has to watch her have sex with another man.

ADULT CONTENT

Penelope got to her feet and crossed to the facilities. Once inside she washed her face and studied her appearance. The image reflected in the mirror above the sink displayed her features, but she barely recognized herself. Stress regarding this bold plan already took its toll in the worry lines around her eyes. Vanity became another useless indulgence in this tense plan.

She took a quick shower for something to do and contemplated which of the seven varieties of pre-packaged meals she'd consume next as she dried her hair. She slipped back into her camisole and put a new pair of panties on.

When she returned to the main room she sniffed the air. Something smelled really good. It was as if the ebony darkness of the blackout had left behind a shadowy delicious scent for her to savor.

What was that? She inhaled deeply once again.

It smelled so magnificent she wanted to discover the source and bury her face in whatever it was. She sniffed the air here and there trying to find the trail to the elusive scent. The search led her to the bed she'd abandoned and then to the vent above. Standing on her tiptoes, after climbing up on the mattress and with hands pressed flat against the wall for balance, Penelope took a deep breath of the breeze coming from the air duct vent.

Ah. Delicious.

There was something scrumptious in the next room and she wanted more. Much more. After quick consideration she determined the scent likely came from a delectable man.

Time to find him and get acquainted.

Penelope leapt off the bed, skipped across the room and hit the button to unlock the door. Once out in the hallway, she followed her nose to the room next door.

She pushed the button, seeking entrance, and door slid open to admit her instantly into a semi-darkened room as if she were expected. Grateful that the way inside to find the delicious man hadn't been locked, Penelope quickly crossed the threshold, closed and locked the door behind her and took another deep lungful of luscious manly aroma.

The overwhelming scent of soap, cologne and this man's lingering raw masculinity rushed into her lungs. The unique fragrance carried through to the very marrow of her bones, touching every nerve in her body along the way with a tingle thrumming her basest desire. Her pussy came alive, demanding unfathomable pleasure as the man on the bed stirred awake. A golden lock of his hair gleamed in the near darkness from a narrow shaft of light in the room.

Half lifting his wide shoulders from the bed, the man turned and shot a drowsy look over one shoulder. A voice gruff with sleep said, "Who are you and what are you doing in my quarters?"

Time to get his clothes off and introduce herself properly. She pulled her camisole over her head and flung it across the room. "I'm Penelope, and I've come to fuck you."

* * * *

Gray had experienced some wild dreams in his past, but the one currently playing out had to be the most outrageous.

"I'm Penelope, and I've come to fuck you," she'd said and flung off her skimpy shirt, which went sailing through the air in the direction of his dresser, revealing the most beautiful set of breasts he'd ever had the pleasure to see naked. Flawlessly molded round globes, sure to fit perfectly in his hands should the opportunity arise to touch them, currently bounced across the room towards him like a private fantasy come to life.

The dim light of his room didn't afford him the detailed pleasure of her nipples, but since she'd started strolling to his bed, he imagined he was about to see them up close and personal in mere seconds.

"Is this a joke?" he muttered as his cock, already stiff with after-slumber arousal, pulsed, hopefully.

"No. And we need to hurry." She hooked her thumbs into the barely-there scrap of panty fabric covering her mound, bent at the waist and shucked those off as well. Her body popped straight again and those perfect breasts bounced closer and closer, making his mouth suddenly water.

"Why do we have to hurry again?" Gray flipped his legs over the side of his bed as she took the final steps to meet him in all her nude glory. And she was glorious.

She lowered her beautiful face until it was even with his. "Because I burn for you. Please. I need to fuck you. Right now." Her eyes stared straight through him, but the glassy sheen gave her aqua gaze a distant aura. As if she didn't see the view directly before her eyes.

Gray stood carefully as she straightened with him remaining very close. He grabbed her slim shoulders as she proceeded to press the full length of her delectable body against him. In the next instant, her fingers unerringly found the stiff length of his cock and squeezed her fist around him like some seductive test of endurance. Even through the fabric layer of his clothing, unabashed pleasure spiked from his shaft, and urgent desire rippled outwardly to every part of his body.

He grunted, "Wait." The prickle of desire she elicited in his cock almost overrode his level-headed danger signal of a strange woman being in his room ready to fuck his brains out.

"I can't wait." She gripped his cock tighter through the flight suit he hadn't bothered to take off before falling into bed. With her titan grip on his cock, he didn't notice her other hand had located the zipper. Not until he heard the sound of the opening zipping down his front and felt the air on his chest.

She released her hold on his cock only to slip her hand beneath the fabric of his now wide open flight suit to grab his shaft with the most unbelievably soft hand he'd ever had caressing his privates.

"God almighty!" A roar followed those two words, wrenched from his lips when she fell to her knees. Gray got a millisecond of warning before her hot, wet mouth closed over the end of his cock and blissful suction progressed.

Siren Publishing, Inc.
www.SirenPublishing.com

LaVergne, TN USA
15 March 2010
176118LV00005B/59/P